Praise for Susan

Elsey Come Home

"Sometimes the structure of a novel so suits its content, so fully allows characters to inhabit the page, that it's hard to imagine any other arrangement. So it is with Susan Conley's twisty, absorbing new novel, with its brief urgent chapters that read like dispatches from near and far. . . . Readers may come away from this book marveling at the small miracle they've just witnessed. . . . Elsey is that rare creation that evokes real life, defies predictability and disarms us at every turn. Conley has taken a jittery pile of loose ends and made a thing of beauty." —*Portland Press Herald* (Maine)

"A beautiful, ethereal piece of writing. . . . Packed with emotional resonance and deftly-turned phrases."
—*The Maine Edge*

"Even within a few paragraphs of this exploration of motherhood and individuality, Elsey's voice and emotional turbulence leap off the page." —*HuffPost*

"Beautifully written. . . . A thought-provoking novel."
—*The Washington Times*

"Conley's prose exudes purpose and rhythm, an unusually lovely combination, creating a rich mood and atmosphere that will have you craving a trip to China."
　　　　　　　　　　　　　　　　　　　—*Fodor's*

"*Elsey Come Home* is a smart, wry, and immersive coming-of-middle-age story of growth and womanhood."　　　　　　　　　　　　　　—Hello Giggles

"[A] well-paced, quietly moving novel. . . . [Elsey's] thoughtful, vulnerable, honest articulation of her pain—told from a distant future vantage point—is what truly drives her story toward resolution."
　　　　　　　　　　　　　　　　—*Shelf Awareness*

"Probing questions about how to balance motherhood, a career, marriage, and a drinking problem resonate throughout Conley's excellent novel. . . . [*Elsey Come Home* is] an honest and astute depiction of the human psyche."　　　　—*Publishers Weekly* (starred review)

"Conley's slim novel illustrates the power of storytelling as a process for healing. What entices and endures here is the voice: dreamy, meditative, hypnotic, and very real."　　　　　　　　　　　　—*Kirkus Reviews*

"Moving."　　　　　　　　　　　—*Southern Living*

"An intimate declaration of independence. . . . Readers will be hard-pressed not to finish the slender volume in one sitting."   —*The Associated Press*

"A quiet, contemplative portrait of a woman searching for herself."   —*Book Page*

"Author of the memoir *The Foremost Good Fortune*, an *O, the Oprah Magazine* 'Top Ten' pick, and the debut novel *Paris Was the Place*, a *People Magazine* Top Pick, Conley returns with a new novel carrying the poignancy and fraught scrape of relationships that characterized them both."   —*Library Journal*

"What a quirky little gem of a book Susan Conley has written. I'm still trying to figure out how she created a character so seemingly lost to herself without losing me in the process. There's genuine alchemy here."
—Richard Russo, author of *Empire Falls*

"*Elsey Come Home* is a thing of wonder and beauty, a novel about faraway places, both internal and external. I read this in one thirsty gulp and through its window was shown certain truths about the joy, pain, and intricacy of marriage and of being. Susan Conley is a magical writer; this book is her magic."   —Mike Paterniti, author of *The Telling Room*

"I love Elsey—her vulnerability, and self-awareness, and her love for her daughters, which permeates the novel. This book is lush with colors, smells, and sounds and has a compulsive, deeply gratifying shape. We're allowed to witness Elsey in all her glory, even when she's unable to see herself clearly." —Lewis Robinson, author of *Water Dogs*

Susan Conley

Elsey Come Home

Susan Conley is the author of the novel *Paris Was the Place* and *The Foremost Good Fortune*, a book that won the Maine Literary Award for Memoir. Conley was raised in Maine, and her writing has appeared in *The New York Times Magazine*, *The Paris Review*, and *Ploughshares*. She has been awarded fellowships from the MacDowell Colony, the Bread Loaf Writers' Conference, the Maine Arts Commission, and the Massachusetts Arts Council. She spent three years in Beijing with her husband and two sons before moving back to Portland, Maine, where she currently lives. She teaches in the Stonecoast Writing Program at the University of Southern Maine.

www.susanconley.com

Also by Susan Conley

The Foremost Good Fortune
Paris Was the Place

Elsey Come Home

· *Elsey Come Home* ·

Susan Conley

Vintage Books

A DIVISION OF PENGUIN RANDOM HOUSE LLC

NEW YORK

FIRST VINTAGE BOOKS EDITION, NOVEMBER 2019

The Library of Congress has cataloged the Knopf edition as follows:
Name: Conley, Susan, 1967– author.
Title: Elsey come home / Susan Conley.
Description: First edition. | New York : Alfred A. Knopf, 2018.
Identifiers: LCCN 2017058737 (print) | LCCN 2018001187 (ebook)
Subjects: LCSH: Man-woman relationships—Fiction. | Domestic fiction.
Classification: LCC PS3603.05365 (ebook) |
LCC PS3603.05365 E47 2018 (print) | DDC 813/.6—dc23
LC record available at https://lccn.loc.gov/2017058737

Vintage Books Trade Paperback ISBN: 978-0-525-56255-9
eBook ISBN: 978-0-525-52099-3

Book design by M. Kristen Bearse

www.vintagebooks.com

Printed in the United States of America
10 9 8 7 6 5 4 3 2 1

To Tony, Thorne, and Aidan

Elsey Come Home

· I ·

About a year ago my husband handed me a brochure for a retreat in a nearby mountain village. We were standing in our Beijing kitchen while the girls played make-believe dog at our feet. The brochure was more like a handmade pamphlet—four pieces of white computer paper folded in the middle and stapled three times along the crease. There was a grainy photo of a cement terrace on the cover, and a more alarming photo of people sitting in a room with their eyes closed, and text under the photos that explained something called "a day of silence" and yoga and the chance for participants to reinvent themselves. My husband, Lukas, told me these things would make a good week's vacation for me, and he smiled while I looked at the photos, but it was a distant smile.

He went back to his bowl of rice, and I pressed myself against the edge of our stove until my lower back hurt, and I felt so lonely I almost cannot say. I knew if I went to this village, the week would pass slowly and I'd be changed, and that this was the point of him sending me there, but also that Lukas and I might not ever find each other again.

I'd recently had a small surgery with my thyroid, and the Chinese doctor said I would get better, and he was right and so I did. But I'd been in and out of hospitals that previous winter, and when I was home I lay on the couch while Lukas and the girls continued on with their lives. Myla was eight. Elisabeth was seven. They sweetly cleared their plates and cups from the table and put them in the dishwasher upside down. Lukas often read the bedtime stories, and I saw he was trying hard to help me, but that I wasn't needed as much as I thought, and that I must learn how to be a different kind of mother. A different kind of wife. It still feels like that now while I write this. That I cannot go back to the way I was before.

I will also say that when Lukas handed me the brochure in our kitchen I didn't know how to be in a marriage. A real marriage. I'm not sure he did, either. He was from Denmark and had lived in Beijing for fifteen years, making music, and he stormed about the government's crackdown on journalists and rising nationalism, but I'm not sure he'd ever learned how to really listen.

The day before I left for the retreat we took the girls downtown to a Japanese restaurant called Hatsune, which is lined with dark wood and tatami and serves large ceramic bowls of ramen and a sweet, sticky white rice Myla and Elisabeth love. After the rice got served I told the girls I was going away for the week to a tiny village called Shashan, and they stared at me with their grave eyes and clouds of hair. Then the fresh lemon sodas arrived, and neither of them seemed to register my announcement again, even though it was a rare announcement because I hardly ever left them. They played tic-tac-toe with a small pad of paper and pens I'd brought in my bag, and got up to look at the oversized catfish in the aquarium.

During the meal Elisabeth politely asked for a mayonnaise sandwich even though Hatsune was her favorite restaurant in Beijing, and she has always hated mayonnaise and refused to eat anything with mayonnaise on it. When we got home, Lukas made her the mayonnaise sandwich, and I stayed with her in the kitchen while she ate it so Lukas could put Myla to bed. There are two steel stools with black matte leather seats at the end of the stone counter, and Elisabeth and I sat on these while she ate the whole sandwich, which became, I think, a kind of statement. Her long hair was tucked behind her ears, which saved it from getting in the mayonnaise, and she didn't say anything else about my leaving for the mountains.

When Elisabeth was done with the sandwich, I walked her to her room and she lay on her bottom bunk, and I hadn't closed the curtains yet, so we could still see the skyline and the enormous Chinese TV building so famous people come from around the world to look at it. From our apartment it resembles a pair of gray pants. So big I cannot even begin to explain it, and Elisabeth is often in awe of this building. Me too. How could people even get inside that building?

We live downtown in a high-rise near the most gigantic train station. When we moved here just before Myla was born, I circled the train station on my map with indelible marker so when I got lost I could take out my map and try to find my way home.

Elisabeth rolled over on her stomach in the bed. "Imagine," she said, "if you spoke wolf language. I mean really spoke it. Would you live with the wolves and leave your mother and father and never come back?"

She often asked me questions that involved leaving our

family, and I didn't want her to leave our family, and I told her this. Then I said, "Living with wolves would be exciting, and if you didn't like it you could come back."

She looked at me like this was an acceptable answer, and I felt I'd passed a test, which is how I often felt with Elisabeth. Like she was administering a series of small philosophy exams, which were essential I pass in order to be allowed to continue being her mother.

I stood and pulled the blue curtains closed. This was more curtain than I'd encountered in a room, because the picture window was that big. A sliver of light from the noodle house below cut through the gap between the curtains and fell on the rug, and Elisabeth often said it looked like the scar on Harry Potter's forehead.

The rug was hard like turf because it was laid down over concrete, and I'd never seen so much concrete before in my life until I lived in China. Elisabeth asked me what God I believed in, and I'm not sure if this interrogation was already happening before I had the thyroid surgery, but it threw me, because I often asked myself the same question privately. I told her I believed in the God of Family. "You know. The God who keeps families together forever and ever, so they are never apart." Lying was the thing she disliked most of all, but I used to believe it was a way to spare her.

"But what do you really believe in, Mom?"

I smiled for how well she knew me. She'd already changed into the blue sweat suit, because she required being fully dressed for school before she got out of bed in the morning, and I no longer argued with her about this. But it was quite hot in her room and her face was flushed.

"Because I believe when you die," she said, "you go to heaven for thirty years and then you come back as a cheetah because you want to be that fast."

"Okay. Well, what I believe in is my love for you. That's what I believe."

I was trying to calm her mind so she'd be able to sleep. I could still mostly get away with naming my emotions for her explicitly. Maybe they were emotions I couldn't fully name with my husband. I feared once she got just a little older, it would be over and she wouldn't let me speak these things any longer, which has turned out to be mostly true. But there was this sweet time when I got to say them, and it has meant a lot.

Sometimes the streetlights outside her room flickered, and they began doing it then—blinking on and off, and the light landed on the strip of rug underneath the gap in the curtain and made the shapes. "Let's go to sleep now," I said.

I wanted her to sleep so I could pack. I also wanted a drink. I'd begun wanting one every night that winter after I put the girls to bed. I can't fully account for it, but I will say that it didn't feel like anything really happened during those days until I had a drink. I wasn't painting, and I wasn't with the girls doing what some people call parenting, because I was so often on the couch after the surgery. The girls tested me, and I tired more easily. They were still young and wanted things from me, as they should. Food and kisses. I gave them all of this.

I'd certainly drunk before my surgery, but never with intention. And now I thought I might be sicker than the doctors had said, and I was too in a hurry to return to my private conversation with the world about this. It sounds odd. My fear. I was slowly getting better but I couldn't stop the worries, and I thought it was a secret how afraid I'd gotten.

You hear it and don't understand when women say they lost themselves, because it seems overdone, and there are four hundred million people in China living on a dollar a day, so cry me a river.

There's a small, fetid canal outside our apartment where a handful of old men from the hutong fish for carp and catfish. Elisabeth became fixed on these men out our window and often made us walk to the canal to watch them. She was a willful child like this and could take up a lot of the day, but I had no excuse for not painting in the two years leading up to my illness. What I will say is that I couldn't understand how to be obsessed with my children and obsessed with my painting at the same time. I thought both called for obsession. I had a narrow view of the world and I was younger then, but really I was naïve.

· 3 ·

That night I kissed Elisabeth all over her smooth face and
went into Myla's room, which is across the hall and painted
tangerine and looks out over the playground with the shoddy
trampoline the maintenance men recently put up. Myla is
older than Elisabeth, and I used to think older meant easier,
but now I see what you think is hard about your children
changes, and you never have a chance to fall into a pattern
of response. If you don't remind yourself almost every day,
you'll focus only on the hardness and soon their childhoods
will be over. Poof.

I lay down in Myla's bed with her, and she twirled her hair
and asked if she could come with me. Her hair is the color of
caramelized sugar and shorter and finer than Elisabeth's, and
it may be the one thing that gives Myla power over Elisabeth.

I said I didn't think it would work for her to come.

"What if I can't find you there?"

"It's late," I said.

"What if it snows and you get stuck?"

"It hardly ever snows in Beijing. And not in April."

"But you're going to the mountains. What if there's a blizzard and I can't get to you?" Myla wore a cotton nightgown with white ruffles and a Peter Pan collar like the nightgowns my sisters and I used to wear, and this made me softer with her.

I began doing pai-pai, which is the method of Chinese backrub that our ayi, a middle-aged former tour bus guide named Sunny, taught me to do with the girls before I went out at night. We rarely went out, maybe twice a month, but for several years this was enough to send Myla into a fit.

It got so that she'd ask me every morning if I was going out, and when I was honest and told her yes, I was, it made things worse because she'd perseverate on my leaving. Then I tried not telling her I was leaving until I walked out the door, and she'd shriek and throw herself at me so violently I wanted to lie down on the floor with her and cry. I know it's not uncommon for children to fixate on a parent like this for a time, and it's better now and I can see it more clearly, but I wonder what was so important about going out back then that I couldn't stay home.

I told Myla she could always get to me, but I meant it in an abstract way, which is problematic with an overly rational child. I kept doing pai-pai—lightly patting the space between her shoulder blades until I could feel her drifting to sleep, and I repeated myself. "You can always get to me."

I'd lost weight by then, and the tendons in my neck seemed to protrude because my neck was too thin, and I thought I looked much older. I had low confidence, and when I got a small cut on my finger or a scrape on my leg that seemed like nothing at first, it wouldn't heal and this worried me, too. In the photo taped to Myla's bedroom mirror, we're riding a metal chairlift up a mountain east of the city with the Buddhist temple and five hundred stone stairs on top. Myla's head is in my lap, and I hold on to her shoulders with both hands, and even though I was afraid of the height and worried she might fall, I look happy. I am smiling.

"But what if you die there? In the mountains?" she said before she moved fully into sleep. "What if you die and I can't find you?"

I didn't answer except to tell her I loved her, and I kept doing pai-pai. When I left her room, I wanted to sleep the sleep of ten thousand thousand years.

· 4 ·

Our Chinese bed was hard like a bed of wood, and when Lukas climbed in after me he had to bend at his waist and sort of slide in, because he was tall and the bed low to the ground. He had dark wavy hair and a close beard, and the girls' olive skin. He reached his arms around me, and I asked him why he wanted to send me away.

"I'm not making you go," he said. "You know I'm not making you." He smiled at me, and his eyes grew wider. Sometimes his force of will was a thing of beauty and sometimes it was too much.

"If I don't go, you'll hold it against me. So it's sort of like making me." This wasn't true, either. It killed Lukas to be ordinary, but he didn't hold things against people.

He made a certain kind of popular electronic music, and this was the time when his career was changing quickly. He'd built a following that wasn't exactly smiled on by the government, and he was getting more offers from vaguely illegal middlemen to perform.

"This place is for expats," he said. "I've researched it." Foreigners here still called themselves expats, as if it was Shanghai in 1937, before the start of the war.

My husband did a great deal of research. On Chinese tea
and Chinese opera, on Wagner and the lesser-known com-
posers he sampled in recordings. "I think you need to be
gone from the apartment. From the girls and me. We're loud
and take up space."

He had no basis to believe things would turn out well
between us because things had turned out badly for his parents in Denmark, but I didn't understand yet how determined this made him. He kissed me on the lips and looked
at my face, and the light was still on so I could see his brown
eyes, which looked watery—the way they got before he
cried. He was regularly more nakedly emotional than me. I
cried infrequently and mostly over the girls, and I think this
thin barrier between Lukas and the rest of the world was
one reason we were together. For example, when I'd gone
into labor with Myla at the Beijing Hospital, her heartbeat
became irregular and they had to cut me open to get to her.
There was rushing in the operating room and loud voices,
and the Chinese nurses clapped when Myla finally appeared,
and Lukas said he loved me three times. I love you. I love
you! I love you! Each one louder than the next. I felt it, too,
a wave of emotion for him and for everyone in the room,
really, but I didn't know how to name it and was so grateful
he'd said it for me.

So I understood in our bed that he wanted me to tell him

things would be okay between us, but when you haven't said what you feel for a long time, you'll go to lengths to continue not to. I waited, and he turned off the light, and we lay on our backs under the sheet, and I could feel the distance between us and couldn't close the gap, and this amazed me. It wasn't like other distances that can sometimes preserve our marriage, and I didn't know how I'd make my way back to him.

He turned and pressed his face into my neck and kissed me on the collarbone. "The village may be a place," he said, "that will help with the drinking."

He kept tucking a piece of my hair behind my ear while he talked. Tucking my hair and kissing my ear, and I could see he thought there were reasons for my drinking he could fix. Practical reasons, and I wished I believed him. Up until then he hadn't mentioned the drinking. It's pretty common that people in the throes of other people's drinking don't talk about the drinking. You think the drinking is going to get used, but no one dares take the pistol down off the wall and fire it.

He kissed my ear again and held me tight across my rib cage. "This place, Shashan," he said, "will get you some rest. Then you'll come back and be better."

· 5 ·

In the morning Myla came into my bathroom to brush her teeth because she insisted on using our giant bathroom, which was made mostly of the white marble found everywhere in China. I'd pulled a turtleneck sweater over my head, and my hair was still tucked into the neck of the sweater. "You look like a different mommy," she said. "You don't look like my mommy at all." Her face became very worried.

Then Elisabeth lost her first tooth and came running into the bathroom to show us. Lukas kissed her fist that held the tooth and put Elisabeth on his shoulders for a victory lap around the apartment. She held the tooth up in the air, and no one asked about me leaving for Shashan or seemed to have any memory of the Japanese restaurant the night before.

We got the girls set for school, and Lukas came to me by the front door in the hall and put his arms around my waist. I'd already told him that morning how afraid I was to go to the village, and he said he knew this and still thought it was a good idea that I do it. I think we both understood I should do something. But maybe not yoga, which I'd hardly ever tried, and maybe not a week in the mountains where I didn't talk for whole days.

He walked the girls on the concrete path through the gardens to the school bus, and I took my canvas bag and went down to the parking garage under our building and saw my marriage reflected in our car window. An older Chinese man sat in a wooden booth by the garage exit ramp, keeping track of parking spaces, and I smiled at him, and the man waved in the most optimistic way. I didn't call Lukas on my cell phone to tell him I'd seen our marriage in the driver's window, even though he was probably back in the apartment and I should have called, but it felt too early. I hadn't gotten to Shashan yet, and I thought I was already better. Lukas wouldn't have taken me seriously if I said I'd seen our marriage then. I still to this day don't think he would have believed me.

I got in the car and began driving. It's sweltering here in the summer and bone cold in the winter, but in spring the sky can be blue and high like a circus tent, which it was the day I drove to the mountains. It has been my great luck to live here, and also my reprieve in some ways. I made it to the Fourth Ring Road with the one-speed bicycles and rickshaws and Audi sedans, and it may sound counterintuitive because things were as bad as they'd been in my marriage, but I'd seen my marriage in the window before I unlocked my car, and I thought this was all that mattered, that I'd seen it.

I drove three hours into the low mountains that form a soft brown ring around the northeastern edge of the capital and parked in a grassy clearing and began climbing. Lukas hadn't said it was crucial I go, but I felt it was crucial and that things in my marriage were at stake I couldn't easily identify. After thirty minutes or so of walking I came to a concrete terrace where foreigners sat drinking tea at a round plywood table. I was so happy for having made it that I looked out over the mountain valley and imagined I could see China's coast, which becomes round south of Shanghai like a well-fed hen. The pine trees were not unlike the pine trees in Maine where I grew up, and this comforted me, too. But then I got the lurching stomach I've had the two times I've ridden the rickety roller coaster in Beijing, and I thought, "My God what have you done to end up on this terrace and how can you get home?"

The word "terrace" is too fancy, because it was more of a scrabbly concrete yard that extended over the side of the mountain and the astounding view. An awning made from wide sheets of green plastic hung over the concrete and caused the air underneath to get really hot. It was May by then and the chestnut shells hadn't turned green yet, but summer was coming up off the desert, and I loved the heat in China and walking with the girls outside our apartment building to buy the little candied hawthorns on sticks.

A retired middle-school teacher named Mr. Liu and his wife, Mrs. Liu, owned the terrace and the dilapidated stone house and the rooms where we slept. Mr. Liu's dark hair had a bird crest in front, and he limped when he brought me to the table where the yoga teacher stood and said he was happy to see me. I didn't know what to say back. His Western name was Justice, and he had hair down to his waist that smelled of oil the villagers pressed from the apricot trees. His skin was polished like walnuts, and he was truly a beautiful man. He was also owner of the Yoga Station in Beijing and lead singer of a metal thrash band called We Can't Stop Kissing One Another that played at the Modernista in the Baochao Hutong on Saturday nights, and Lukas and I had seen him there years ago before the children, when we still went out to hear music. But I'd only met Justice when I took one desperate class at his studio to try and prepare for the week, so I didn't really know him.

I sat at the table with my bag at my feet, and Justice passed me a plastic thermos of tea. Then I looked at the faces around me and was nervous because I was going to have to talk to these people. A French man named Andre sat closest to me and seemed to use a hair oil that made his hair wavy and wet at the same time, and when he kissed me on both sides of my face I know I blushed from his affection. I didn't like to be with groups of strangers. Who does? I worried that all of them at the table—Justice, and Andre, and the older-looking New Zealand woman, and a younger Tahitian woman who said her name was Tamar—were probably what they called yogis. People who did a great deal of yoga. This was a terrifying thought, because I hadn't done yoga for years, except the time in Justice's studio the week before, which hadn't gone well.

Mrs. Liu wore pancake makeup and a pink Mickey Mouse T-shirt and hummed while she cooked the pork in an open canteen on the right side of the terrace. When she finished a dish, Mr. Liu jogged it to the table. There was lo mein with pork, and bright green bok choy, and purple cabbage, and local mushrooms with celery slivers. Everything on the terrace—the wooden canteen, the warped plywood table and plastic chairs—had the feeling of imminent decay, but the Lius were so prone to laughter it was hard not to feel a little festive. I didn't know if it was put-on laughter or real. If I looked up past the Lius' house, I could see pieces of the Great Wall along the tops of the mountains, and this excited me so much, though I still can't say why.

Down below, the valleys were different shades of greens, and I could see the groupings of stone rooftops. The mountains behind the houses were stacked on top of one another so the land looked ancient and mystical and otherworldly.

I'd left my girls for this village. My sister Margaret had died when she was the age Myla was now, and her death became the dividing line for me, so that my life was in two parts. I can't recall anyone who's made me laugh the way Margaret did, and I couldn't see it then, but I was guarding my girls too much in China. Keeping watch over them for signs of danger.

A Chinese woman appeared at the top of the path, which was surprising because locals don't often go to the places where the expats go. Justice stood when he saw her and whispered in her ear, and I decided they were lovers, though this turned out not to be true. She wore drapey, expensive-looking silk, and the bones of her face were delicate and close to the surface. After she sat down at the table, we spun the platters on the glass lazy Susan like we do at the banquets in the capital, and I felt silly doing this on the mountainside and wanted to go home and didn't feel festive anymore.

It seemed like everything I knew before in my life was over. My bed. The gray sectional couch. My husband and girls. The dirt road behind our high-rise. The village looked from another century, quiet and separate, and I didn't belong and was too far away from my girls and unsteady. I wanted to call them so badly. I couldn't corner what my marriage had become, and it was so surprising that my life had arrived at this point where I was out of reach, and I almost couldn't bear it.

· 7 ·

A woman I knew from Beijing made it to the terrace wearing black spandex and carrying a Starbucks cup and seemed about to throw her cell phone over the side of the mountain. "Why won't you work?" she yelled into the phone.

Tasmin lived near the top of the expat pecking order and was frenetically busy in the city. Both her long black hair and neck were thicker than you might expect from someone so thin. I was nervous on the mountain. I've said that already. And I didn't do well with strangers, but until Tasmin got there I hadn't realized how attached I was to the idea of not knowing anyone in Shashan. I was trying to become someone else. Or to lose the person I'd become. My heart wasn't broken yet, but I thought I'd broken Lukas's heart.

Tasmin wrapped her arms around my neck so she was partly strangling me and seemed to be in the act of taking something from me, but I was almost glad for her affection now that my girls were far away and couldn't smother me in their kisses.

"You should have told me you were coming, Elsey." The skin on her face was milk-white and her eyes almost opaque. "I could have had my driver pick you up."

She and her British husband were the money behind the new penthouse apartments at the luxury mall near the embassy road, and Tasmin had bought several of my early paintings, which plagued me because I was indebted and often didn't understand how to act around her. Her boys were the same age as Myla and Elisabeth, and they were very physical boys the last time we'd seen them at Tasmin's garden party, where they'd wrestled in the grass with Elisabeth. But I don't understand boys. I only know about girls.

Tasmin patted the bun on top of my head, and I smiled a pained smile at her but she didn't see that it was pained. She didn't see many things about me. I had a way of appeasing people back then, by appearing to think what they wanted me to think. I did this so they would leave me be. Did I also appease my husband? A marriage, then, based on small acts of omission? It's frustrating to remember how I was, but I thought it was easier.

"We need to fatten you up. And Christ." Tasmin touched the pile on top of my head again. "There's so much hair up here it's like a Russian novel."

The terrace shifted under the gushing force of her will, and many things about myself felt inadequate. My long, unruly brown hair. The faded red tank top I used to run in at college. No one runs in Beijing. The sky outside is often low to the ground and soupy. People belong to gyms. An explosion of gyms. And I could tell if I wasn't disciplined, Tasmin would keep me from doing the work I'd been sent to Shashan to do, which was, I suppose, to develop a method to make me more user-friendly to my family.

My left arm began to feel like someone was stabbing me with a steak knife, and I had a hard time paying attention to Tasmin, because I was focused on the radiating pain that centered around my left elbow. I hadn't talked about this new pain with Lukas, because it had come out of nowhere, and I didn't think it was connected to my previous illness. We'd been through enough, and I didn't want to scare him more than I already had.

Ulla came up the path next and sat at the table. She was taller than any other woman I knew in Beijing, and I was surprised she had time to be in the mountains. She'd been recently divorced and had no children and was on loan from the University of Stockholm's biology department to help build a massive organic farming initiative in North Korea. She flew to Nampa months at a time to oversee implementation, and I knew soon she'd be seen striding across the mountain with her spikey hair after some rare bird.

I used to pretend to be more ambitious around Ulla than I really am, because I wanted her to respect me, and I wanted a friend to belong to in China other than my husband. But really I'm someone who likes to paint at night in my underwear and take small pulls of scotch.

The woman from New Zealand was named Tree, and she began arguing with Tasmin over the best foot massage parlor in Beijing. Tree wore a slab of turquoise on a thin chain around her neck and was older like me. Maybe forty. With a pretty, leathery face and wavy hair that were both partly deceiving. I've also had discussions about foot massage in China, so I wasn't above them in any way. Foot massage is a serious thing here. I just felt wrong after I had these discussions, because there were more important things in China to argue about. A few years earlier I'd read the journal of a poet named May Sarton who lived on the Maine coast while I was growing up there. When May Sarton came home from dinner parties, she wrote down each thing she'd said at the party that made her feel badly about herself, and this stayed with me—how freely she must have talked at the dinners and how hard she was on herself when she got home—and I didn't want to become like her, someone who seemed at times to hate herself.

Tree said China was in her blood, and she wanted more than anything to fall in love with a Chinese man. The papery skin around her eyes crinkled when she smiled. "Justice is a fine specimen."

We all stared more closely at her after that. Or at least I did, because she didn't censor herself, which excited me. I don't think we knew what to do with her honesty, because we'd been on the terrace only a short time and were still learning how we belonged there or didn't.

"No, I don't really mean that," Tree said. "Don't listen to me. I think out loud too much."

"Drinks, please!" Tasmin snapped her fingers, which broke Tree's spell, and everyone at the table laughed.

"What is this thing called the Talking Circle?" Tasmin read the yoga brochure out loud, and people were sort of half listening to her while they finished their dinner, but this didn't bother her the way it would have bothered me. I could have never commandeered the table like that.

Before anyone could answer, two boys and a girl made it to the terrace, the boys in black eyeglasses and hair mousse that caused their bangs to stick up, and the girl's hair dyed white and shaved around her left ear and its piercings. They sat in the plastic seats, and the blonder boy took a fierce drag on his cigarette and asked Justice for the Wi-Fi password. Justice shook his head and told him there wasn't Wi-Fi in Shashan and the girl shoved the boy with her shoulder.

"We're in the mountains in China, for fuck's sake," she said. "No Wi-Fi." She had a small metal bar through the cartilage of her nose, which moved up and down when she spoke, and the other, darker-haired boy in the blue hoodie smiled and rolled his eyes.

I knew about the Talking Circle. I'd studied the brochure for stretches of time on the couch in my living room, while my children were at school and I climbed out of a headache.

"'A time,'" Ulla read out loud over Tasmin's shoulder, "'when people talk about what comes up for them during yoga that day.' Oh, mother of God."

No one said anything after that for a few seconds, and Ulla's scratchy voice hung over the table.

Tasmin said, "Talking Circles make me want to go get a drink."

I'd already decided to give up drinking that afternoon, but I got that feeling I sometimes get in China that shots of grain alcohol are going to appear soon on bamboo trays, and I couldn't say whether or not I'd drink one.

Ulla and the woman named Tamar began to speak to each other—unconnected things that spread to the people next to them—and there was a disjointed discussion about yoga mats and how long it had taken Andre and Tree to drive to Shashan in the white minivan Justice had rented in the city. It became difficult to follow. I'm not sure which worried me more, the yoga or the Talking Circle, because I didn't know if I could do either. I was stupid for having come to the mountains. What would I get out of it? I wanted to drink. So badly I wanted to drink.

"Taxi!" Tasmin stood up. "Can I get a taxi out of here, Justice?" She smiled at him and sat back down. "Does anyone have a cigarette for me?"

Andre handed over his soft pack of Yuxis. He smoked, too?

"There is a God!" Tasmin winked at me.

I didn't have anyone else in my life who winked at me, and it was the strangest thing. I had to fight the urge to become someone other than myself. Someone who winks back, for example. Or smokes. Maybe I was unfair to Tasmin, but she seemed to have a disregard for where we really were: on a small forgotten mountain in China that appeared to have little electricity. How can I explain? It was an expat trick the way she was able to suspend belief that we were there living in China and to negate the whole country, while also navigating it and making it her own.

Ulla laughed her deep, manly laugh and looked at her watch. "We go now?"

"Soon." Justice looked at her and up at the sky like he was reading the clouds, but really I think he was waiting for the Chinese woman to finish her meal. She appeared to be a slow eater.

Ulla wasn't satisfied. You could tell. She didn't like to not be the one in control. Maybe she would make the yoga serious. I needed it to not be a joke. I thought I'd have to leave Shashan then and go home. It was like a panic attack, and I almost talked myself into it. To leave.

10

An American man was last to arrive, and he took the chair on the right of the Chinese woman and said his name was Hunter and that he was in coal mining. I didn't know anyone else who stated their line of business like this. The Chinese woman told him her name was Mei and that she was from Beijing. Then she snapped a drumstick off one of the chickens and began eating.

We were twelve. I counted ten foreigners and two nationals, if you included Justice, and I moved my chair closer to Tasmin's, but we still barely fit. I remember sort of following the conversation, but I was worked up, which is what happens if you've spent several weeks lying on a couch in a loft-style apartment in downtown Beijing willing yourself to get better and are asked to perform yoga.

For a long time the question for me had been whether to paint or be a mother. But I think there's no choice. Or that the choice is a myth. Because once the girls arrived they took over my heart, and now I'd left them in the city because I could not seem to parent them. Little grasses grew in the cracks on the patio, and the concrete had chipped away completely in places, which made it harder to move my chair back when we stood and followed Justice to our rooms.

I was relieved to finally be doing something. Tasmin's room was the only one actually attached to the Lius' house. Ulla's was next to Tasmin's. Then mine and Hunter's and Mei's and the others'. Justice told the two boys and girl from England they would have to sleep on the kang inside the Lius' house, because there were no rooms left. The kang was the platform bed in the Lius' living room that looked sort of like a wooden throne when I saw it from the front window. This would have thrown me. If Justice had told me I was sleeping in the kang, I think it would have given me permission to go home.

My room had a white laminate door like in cheaper motels in the city, and a picture window, and a double bed with a quilted blue polyester spread. The bathroom was like a cramped phone booth, with shiny one-inch white tiles and an open shower that soaked everything in the room when I turned it on. I placed my bag on the bed and changed into the wide-legged pants I'd bought at the martial-arts school in Sanlitun. Then I went outside and found the group on the far side of the terrace preparing to walk to what Justice called the yoga house. I knew Ulla and Tasmin expected me to walk to the yoga house with them. But if I did this, I understood I'd have to walk everywhere with them in Shashan and I can't say how much I didn't want to walk everywhere with them.

I must have known the retreat was my chance to keep my

husband, and that if I didn't change, he would leave me. I hadn't said this clearly to myself before, but I knew he eventually would. I made sure I was one of the last to leave the terrace, so I ended up behind Mei in the line of walkers. It was like I was in middle school the way I strategized, and this took effort, but nothing like the effort it had taken me to get to Shashan.

Instead of following the path to the parking area, we turned onto a second path past the backs of several brick houses with donkeys tied up in the dirt yards. The path was well worn, but you wouldn't have known it existed if Justice hadn't been leading us, and it was like we were almost inside these houses, the path was so close to them.

When I'm nervous, I also have a reflex that's more like a compulsion, and I see my younger sister Margaret's face, so then I felt even more cut off from my children. I wasn't used to being without them, and I tried to balance being a mother with being Margaret's sister and still not understanding what was called for in this life after she was gone.

The man in Beijing who I pay to ask me questions once told me that I didn't know how to name my emotions, and when he and I came to the subject of my sister's death this man asked me, "What do you feel?"

I'd tried to smile at him, because there was this pain, and the man imitated my fake smile, and I hated him for that. Really hated him and almost left him over it, but later I saw he was right and I didn't have words for how I felt, and I needed to do more than smile.

The man asked me to write a history of certain parts of my life in order to try to differentiate the present from the past, and it calls on me to be honest in a way I'm not used to and hasn't been without difficulty. I'm a painter. I know I've said that. It's been my experience to translate life through image and little blasts of unexpected color, and I'm not used to getting to say everything I want to say in one place like this, so I'm unsure what to leave out.

When I first met with the man who I pay to ask me questions, I told him I felt guilty for leaving my girls and driving to Shashan for the week. The man said, "Guilt. Get over it. You don't have time for that luxury now."

11

The houses in Shashan were single-story and wedged into a crease between the two steep mountain faces, and they were old houses. Ancient-looking. With sweet, scalloped stone roofs and the faint odor of rotting pineapple. I may have already said it felt like another century there. The path was steep and rocky and maybe two feet wide. Some of the houses had open wooden pens in the backyards and pigs called sows inside the pens, and some houses had animal sheds attached with corrugated roofs and dogs on metal chains. I couldn't believe the size of the dogs, and I thought that when I got home I'd tell my girls how glad I was the dogs hadn't eaten me.

Myla is my oldest. I've mentioned that. I knew she'd want to know I was safe and coming home soon. She kept track of me, and she wouldn't care about the dogs really. Elisabeth would wonder if the dogs were speaking in dog. She was interested in things like animal language and mystery and was also tied to me but in less obvious ways than Myla.

Several old women came out of their houses to stare at us. They were silent and wraithlike in the gray wool blazers the Chinese grandmothers wear, with pure white hair and creased faces. I felt like a Russian cosmonaut because of my height and my green yoga mat, but I regularly felt like a Russian cosmonaut in China. The path got steeper the lower we went, and there were larger rocks that almost blocked the way, so in certain places it was easier to try to step from rock to rock. Mei wore black sandals with a two-inch wedge heel, and I worried about her shoes and if she would fall on the rocks, and then she did.

"Thank you," she said after I helped her stand. She'd taken off the wig and pulled her long hair back with two purple butterfly barrettes. I hadn't known her hair during dinner was not her real hair, and I liked her real hair better than the wig hair.

"I have never done the yoga before," she said. "I am a very nervous person about the dogs."

The dogs were barking up a storm. "The dogs are tied up," I said. I was surprised she was scared and I wasn't and that she was willing to admit it. I thought it would be the other way around. I took her elbow while she sidestepped down, but it was difficult in the sandals, and she almost fell again.

"I will leave in the morning and go back to Leng and throw things at him," she said. "I am sorry I am swearing." She was not swearing. "I am embarrassed that you have seen me like this."

She had a way of declaring what was right in front of her,

and I could never tell if this was a product of the translation from Mandarin to English, because some of the other Chinese people I knew had this candor, too, and I was drawn to it and it was nothing like what I grew up with.

"At Leng?" I said. "You're mad at Leng?"

I knew a Leng who painted enormous schools of black fish, and when I saw these paintings in Dashanzi where Leng showed, or at exhibits in the national museums, I wanted to buy one. They were ironic and sly and featured many Chinese people swimming in the same direction. Or maybe the fish were meant to be Westerners. It seemed very hard to make political paintings in China like this and also achieve public and critical success. The story went that he'd been shot at Tiananmen Square and had gone into hiding but was later rehabilitated and married to an equally respected artist named Mei, reclusive and rarely seen.

We got to an easier part of the path, and I let go of Mei's arm and we walked almost side by side where the path allowed, and I asked her why she was in Shashan. I'd realized who she was but couldn't fully take her in yet. That she was on the mountain with me. Her most famous paintings were of women in small villages where nothing was quite finished: the women, and the rivers the women sat next to, and the explosions of yellow wildflowers. The sense was of approximation. Of not being willing to fully pin things down and the relief of that. Mei put little poems in the upper corners of the canvas that were commentaries on the early deaths of her parents from poverty and what she called political duress.

I'd seen photos of Mei before, but she looked nothing like the photos, and it took me some time in Shashan to understand this difference and that it was the effect of the wigs she wore.

"No one ever asks me questions," she said. "Thank you." She seemed truly grateful. "I came here because my cousin Justice is helping me leave my husband."

We descended for ten minutes or so until it flattened out in a small dirt clearing in front of the yoga house, which was smaller than most of the other houses and set farther back from the edge of the mountain, with two donkeys in the yard who slept standing up. The whole village appeared cut into the mountainside, with many houses seeming to balance on the edge, and it worked like a tiny city and was purposeful in that way. You could stand outside the yoga house and look up and hold almost all the other houses in the village in your mind at once.

She told me she came from a village where it had been her job to watch the family goat. "I followed the goat up into the hills each day. I am what you say, self-taught." Then she laughed. "I have never been to America and would like to be going there. You should take me." She looked to see what my face was doing. I didn't take her seriously. Many people in China told me they wanted to come to America and didn't mean it. But I was excited that she talked directly to me.

The yoga house had a wooden door with a metal latch, and everyone else had gone inside. Mei touched the barrettes in her hair with each hand and said the reason she was leaving her husband was because he was sleeping with the country's judo champion. I nodded like I understood what she was telling me, but my mind wasn't clear, and I put my hand on her shoulder and pressed it. I didn't say anything else, because it was quiet inside the house and people could hear us. Then I opened the door.

12

"Make yourselves into strong pieces of wood," Justice said, and Tasmin groaned. She was in the front row with Ulla and Tree and Andre. I was in the back with the others. The house was really one large room with three wooden beams across the ceiling, and a dirt floor covered with red Persians. Justice must have lit incense before we got there because the room had a strong smell. He said in order to do plank we needed to prop ourselves up on our hands and the balls of our feet and clench our bottoms and pull our stomachs in, until everything was in a straight line. I looked only at him and tried to forget the people around me, and his voice was kinder than I'd remembered.

I was trying to be inside my body and not in my head, and it was hard and I was self-conscious. I thought of a Halloween party in Maine that my parents had when I was ten, and a friend of theirs came to our porch without clothes on. I'd opened our front door and told Craig McGrath that he was naked, and he said naked was his costume, and I said

I wouldn't wear a costume like that if I were him. He was famous in our town for sailing in the America's Cup, and it seemed on our front porch like he was very comfortable in his body, but I see now that Craig McGrath was drunk.

Not long after this party, many people in our town got divorced, and it became like an epidemic along the river. Women left their husbands, and sometimes left their children. Some of these women hadn't gone to college or didn't finish college because they'd gotten married halfway through and moved to Maine. Maybe it dawned on them what it meant to be vaguely employable and required to live with a man they hardly knew for the rest of their lives. There was also much more snow in Maine than there is now, which made it harder to get through the winters. You had to do something significant if you were from away, like put out a very large forest fire or build a YMCA, before the locals would accept you.

Hallowell was halfway up the state, with double-wide trailers and wooden Capes and saltboxes, and the town was poor and forgotten and also beautiful like Shashan and full of trees. My father was an only child and the first person in his family to go to college, and he left briefly to do this up in Calais, where he met my mother. They came back to Hallowell and bought a square carriage house on loan six miles from the river, where back-to-the-landers lived, and solar house designers and potters and alcoholic tennis instructors, and fourth-generation fishermen.

My parents went to parties at night, and I watched my two

younger sisters while our parents were gone and felt responsible for them and kept things from them so they wouldn't be
scared. Scraping sounds I heard on the porch. Rustling at the
windows. My youngest sister, Ginny, was a baby and slept in
a crib, but my middle sister, Margaret, was two years younger
than me and she stayed up. She was dedicated like that and
didn't want to be left out. I acted as if everything was okay,
but in truth I was very worried for us at night in the woods.

The new people in town from away had parties, and the
locals had parties, and my parents were invited to them all
because my father was a local who'd come back home and
become a bank manager and a woodcarver and an avid gar-
dener. Margaret stood in her flannel nightie and screamed
and banged her hand against the back door when our parents
left for these parties. It was a thick door made of barn wood,
and we had to lock it so she wouldn't run into the driveway
and follow them. Her dark hair flipped up at the ends when
she got sweaty like this, and it was the saddest scream. So I
pretended I wasn't sad and that I didn't want our parents to
stay with us. I thought if I was quiet and pretended what was
happening wasn't happening, I'd save people this way, and I
let Margaret and Ginny help make butterscotch pudding and
we ate it out of the saucepan. Margaret made farting sounds
with her hand under her armpit and did amazing impressions
of our parents when they became very mad at us, and once I
fully wet my pants laughing. Margaret.

I was thirteen, and my parents called it a central nervous
system cancer, which I didn't understand except it sounded

large and central. Ginny understood nothing. I now know that Margaret had the kind that started in the brain and traveled the spinal column and stopped somewhere there. I don't remember junior high, except she lay in bed a great deal, and I smoked pot I got from a tenth-grader on the bus named Steve Grodin who kept it in his backpack. I was on the cross-country team, and I'd smoke in my room down the hall from the room where my sister was resting and go for a run along the river, up past the cemetery and Steve Grodin's house. The pot made me serene. It did not make me sad.

When Steve Grodin asked me to meet him at his father's hunting cabin on the cliffs in the woods behind our houses, I said yes because I wanted to appear fearless, and this is what you did if you were floating and waiting to be saved. I was thirteen. He took off his pants in the slant-roofed loft that you got to by ladder. They were jeans. I have no memory of climbing the ladder. He lay down on top of me, and I don't recall talking. Or the taking off of my pants. I remember my shock, and I don't know how I got him off me, or if I walked home or ran through the April snow.

I went to the state university in Farmington, because it was the only college I applied to. Painting had always been something I did. I had a special love for it, and for my high school art teacher, a sheep farmer named Mrs. Henderson who smoked a pipe and wore motorcycle boots and obtained paint for us when the rest of the school was running out of paper. College was mostly a blur, but I made many oils of famous women painters because Mrs. Henderson sent me to college with a book called Famous Women Painters that saved me. It taught me how to copy, and I didn't know when you copy you reinterpret, even if you don't tell yourself this.

My painting was concerned with the question of what was beautiful. Was I beautiful? I was eighteen and nineteen and twenty. Was life beautiful? Or dying or suffering? Beauty mattered greatly to me in the unearned way that feels distant now. I wasn't often inside my body, and I believed it was important to remain unattached. I began trying not to want anything too much and to hold myself apart, though I didn't see it. I got tattoos, maybe as acts of self-preservation. First on my ankle, and then on my left bum cheek and then on my forearm, and I wish I could say things stopped there.

I met a theatre boy named Cal who walked on his hands next to the creek that runs through Farmington, and he said walking on his hands was an expression of all the emotion he had in his body for me, and I stood in the grass and stared at him and felt something shift in the frozen water of my heart. I wanted to bury myself in this boy, but I couldn't yet. My sister had only been dead eight years.

I moved to Dublin after college and lived with my cousin Emmet and his acoustic band in a squalid boy apartment, and this is where I became a painter. It's a longer story that doesn't matter now, except that I didn't go back to Maine until many years later.

13

Side plank was harder, and Justice said we were supposed to roll over and hold ourselves up on the mat with one arm and the outer edge of one foot. I couldn't do this for long. Tasmin laughed and fell back down on her mat, but Ulla and Andre's faces were very serious, and they looked like they could hold side plank for hours. In triangle pose I was meant to stand sideways with my legs about three feet apart and bend down and reach my right arm to the floor to make a triangle with my body. I could get my hand only as far down as my shin after I straightened my right leg, but I was okay about this.

My mind went to Tommy Miller, an American I'd lived with in Ireland, who was on residency for pediatric neuro-surgery. He smoked French cigarettes and played English Beat albums in our brick apartment near the lake in the north of the city and asked me to marry him. I thought he was insular like me, and I liked that about him—that he didn't need me. For about a year it felt like a marriage, though I see now I didn't know what was called for in a marriage or what a marriage was at all. I think I always knew I'd leave him because I hadn't known him. It was impossible, because I hadn't known myself. The sex and the English Beat were enough to keep me with him, until I left and moved in with the owners of the Montessori school where I worked. A vegan couple in their forties who let me sleep in their den on the corduroy pullout couch and said I was crazy to walk away from Tommy Miller, but I knew this was code for walking away from marriage and babies, and I didn't want either. I wanted to paint.

I took night classes at the local university and did more portraits of women painters: Cassatt, Vanessa Bell, Kahlo. At first I was faithful in my paintings to these women's faces and breasts and hips. Then I left the portraits and began copying the master paintings I saw in the museums, which romanticized the raping of many women, and the casualness of the rapes confused me. My paintings grew more and more abstract. A woman's body became a cloud, which became a storm. I stayed up at night painting in the room with the pullout couch and thought it was possible to make the paintings I most wanted to make and that I shouldn't be afraid of my imagination because it was just my imagination and my confidence soared. In the mornings I was racked with self-doubt and thought I should never paint again.

My teacher at the night classes had a gravelly cough, and when I brought my interpretation of Delacroix into class she said, "And so another master falls, Miss Steele." Then she lit another cigarette and laughed.

I took three paintings to the galleries the next Saturday in a van I borrowed from the preschool owners. I didn't know if the work was any good, but I knew it was different from the work I'd done before, less interested in narrative and more about the color and unexpected shapes. At the third gallery, the owner said he'd take the Delacroix and I started to cry. After that I began to paint more genuinely and it took over my life.

14

Justice asked us to bend at our waists and hang our arms down to the ground, and when I did this my head weighed a thousand pounds. It was relaxing down there. Quiet. My mind went to the music my husband makes, which I have sometimes imagined is stacked like a Beijing skyscraper with a detachable roof. Lush and fabulous to listen to when I was drunk and painting. We met in 2004 when I came to the capital for an exhibit, and my jet lag was like an opiate, though I've never tried opiates. I'd been living alone in an apartment near the University of Dublin, and I'd had a show in Los Angeles and one in New York. Then another. I thought I might always live alone with my paintings.

My first night in China my hosts took me to an EDM show, which is what they call the electronic dance music Lukas makes, and I'd never been to this kind of show before. We were in what was a long rectangular warehouse. Lukas stood on a lit stage with several computers and black consoles, and there were wooden risers on the side of the stage, and this is where I went to stand and watch. He got excited during one of his songs and raised an arm up in the air and danced a little around his computers. He had the thin, boyish features and wiry frame and the same close-shaved beard he has now. His brown hair was longer and moppish in the heat, and he wore dark jeans that appeared to be made of cardboard.

At one point he looked toward the risers and said, "It's a bit warm up here, you know? Would you mind fetching me a glass of water?"

There were other people on the side of the stage, but I thought Lukas looked only at me when he asked for the water, and my stomach flipped. I cannot overstate how happy I was to get him the water. I didn't know the word for water yet in Mandarin, but it seemed universal, and when I asked, the bartender handed me a full glass.

It took some time to carry the water back to Lukas. The people around him were like groupies and were what I would call electronic music people who came to see what songs he played. It's a different world, electronic music. I grew up in the woods on Joni Mitchell songs that tell stories. Lukas once told me he grew up on imported rap music in a block of brick apartment buildings subsidized by the Danish government, but in general he doesn't like to talk about his past.

The people around me on the risers were quiet. Some had come to the club only to see Lukas, not to dance, but I didn't understand this yet, or electronic music. It sounded seductive and almost kitschy and reminded me of a different

kind of music I used to listen to from the late 1970s. Ooz-
ing synthesizers and drum machines, and guitars and bass
and brass. The sea of people on the dance floor waited for
the waves of sound or swells, and no one really talked while
they waited, and it was intimate in this way and also sensual.
I couldn't get over that. How moved everyone was by the
music and by being there.

I handed Lukas the glass of water. He had on oversized
black headphones like a helmet, and I waited to see if he'd
forgotten me. It was important in a way, because I'd made
the effort to go to the bar, but it was also going to be easy
to make it a throwaway moment. If he didn't remember I'd
gone to get the water, my plan was to walk into the dancers
and find my hosts. I was jet-lagged enough to be open to
whatever happened. He thanked me loudly because I don't
think he could hear himself well, and when he smiled I knew
it was genuine, and in this way I understood an essential part
of him and that he saw me as a real person, so I stayed.

After he was done, we took a cab to his apartment in a
mid-rise near the Workers Stadium, and I sat on his formica
counter. He pulled my silk tank top over my head and then
gently tugged off my skirt, which was high-waisted and tight,
so he had to kneel on the floor and slide it off my hips and
then my underpants. He's a considerate lover like that, and
we didn't leave his apartment except to get steamed shrimp
dumplings, which we ate in bed while we watched a Gong
Li movie. In between the dumplings and the movie we made
more love, and I didn't know that you could make love three

times in a night. I mean, I knew it, but I hadn't done it, and we got no sleep, and I haven't ever felt that reckless again.

On my fourth day in Beijing he said he wanted to drive me to a lake on the west side of the city near the summer-houses for the Communist Party officials and remove my clothes and swim with me. He was completely generous with his heart, and it was all unexpected and perfectly logical. He drove me to the lake and took off my clothes in his little car in a small wooded area near a teahouse with a talking parrot. I never left Beijing after that. I never went back to Dublin. I had some of my things shipped.

15

"Once upon a time," Justice said, "there was a great Daoist philosopher named Zhuangzi who fell asleep by a river and dreamt he was a butterfly, flitting from leaf to leaf. When the philosopher woke, he didn't know if he was a man dreaming he was a butterfly, or if he was a butterfly dreaming he was a man, but he didn't worry the distinction. This is what I want for you in Shashan," he said. "To become the butterfly."

I sat up and nodded, but really I had no idea what he was talking about. I just knew I wanted to be like him. Calm. He said when he was a teenager he'd been a novice at a monastery in Burma, where his teaching involved twenty hours of sitting meditation a day. Now he wanted for us to begin the Talking Circle, where each of us would take a stone from the middle of the rug and say something about our feelings and put the stone back.

I wasn't ready for this. I thought the Talking Circle might be better for a Saturday Night Live skit and that Lukas would smile to know he'd sent me away for a week to a place where

I was meant to speak to strangers while holding a black stone in my lap. I was also afraid if I took the stone, I'd talk about my thyroid surgery, which was pretty easy to do once I got going, except I regretted it afterward, like May Sarton.

Tree went first. "I lived for a year with a guru in the Himachal Pradesh in northern India," she said. "As far away from people as I could be. I spent six months in silence and felt very close to the ground. At times all I wanted was to sink back into the earth."

She spoke clearly and quietly and never wavered, and I'm not sure anyone in the yoga house knew what to do after she finished. Most of us looked at our bare feet or maybe at some spot on the plaster wall behind Justice or at the brass cup with the burnt incense sticks. What Tree had said was quite serious and dire, and I decided to block it out, even though this was what Lukas thought was my biggest problem in life, blocking things out.

Mei surprised me by going next, and for a minute she seemed like she was in a daze and stared at the stone in her lap. Then her face became blank. "I did not know how hard the poses would be," she said. "It isn't good to smoke cigarettes and try to do the yoga."

Tasmin stood and took the stone and sat back down. "Seriously?" she said, and locked eyes on Ulla, who was to my mind the best at yoga and could go from one pose to the next while most of us seemed to not understand what a Sun Salutation was.

"I want to do handstands." Tasmin smiled. "I came to learn

handstands and I won't leave until I do them." It was pretty much what I expected from Tasmin, because she didn't seem encumbered by life or to have any real ambivalence.

Justice nodded at her, and more of the horrible waiting began.

At some point I knew I'd have to get up and take the stone and talk, but I couldn't see how I was going to accomplish any of these things. The acrid sweat I get when I'm extremely nervous started in my armpits. Talking seemed like a matter of adrenaline, and that you got the stone when you couldn't bear the waiting any longer. When I finally stood, I had no idea what I was going to say.

16

"I had to get out of the city," I said. "Because I think I may have arm cancer." I didn't have arm cancer. My God, what was I saying and what was arm cancer? My arm hurt, this was true. But I hadn't been able to stop myself from saying the lie. This seemed to be part of the problem—my complete lack of control. As soon as I said it, I was sick of myself and didn't know how I'd dig myself out of my hole. I stood and put the stone back on the rug, and after that it was quiet in the house again.

Then Andre took the stone and said, "I would like to say that I don't think it was sensitive for Tree to have talked earlier about wanting to die by climbing back into the earth when Elsey is clearly trying hard to live."

Tree cried and said she hadn't known, and I defended her to the group and regretted what I'd confessed and asked them not to change what they planned to say in the Talking Circle because of me.

"It's important," I told them, "for you to be honest." And

I felt truthful when I said this and a little bit like I was still in the Saturday Night Live skit.

Andre said he came to the mountains every year for four reasons: "One. The day of silence." He put his right pointer finger up in the air. "Two. Clarity. Three. Self-knowledge. And four. Peace of mind. Because I fly often and always need the peace of mind." He exhaled slowly and loudly. Four fingers up in the air. I hadn't seen how well groomed he was until then or that his athletic clothing matched and was made of bamboo or some newer wicking material. "These four things are what my yoga teacher teaches me every year, and I thank you for them, Justice." He bowed his head to Justice, and Justice bowed back, and Andre walked to the center of the circle and put the stone down.

Tamar took the stone after Andre and said her husband had recently died in an accident in Southern China. Her long, dark curls fell in front of her shoulders, and she showed so much love for the dead man and cried so hard for him that I began crying for him too and for Tamar and then for Lukas. Tasmin was also crying, and Andre. Again I wanted to go home and tell Lukas I was already better, even though part of me knew this wasn't close to being true. I couldn't imagine a whole week up there. I thought that I'd miss my children to the point I'd be physically sick and have to drive away.

Ulla picked up the stone and said in her heavy Swedish accent that she was looking for evidence of the ephemeral in Shashan. She talked like she was trying to win an argument the way she annunciated last syllables of words and last words of sentences. "It is like a marriage, how we grow the food and care for the land." Then she shrugged. "But I come here to the mountains for the faith."

It had never occurred to me before that Ulla was a spiritual person. I'd always thought she was locked in by the biology of plants, and self-sufficient because she didn't need anything from anyone.

Maeve, the punkish girl with white hair, went next and said her father had found her in bed with a girl in Auckland when she was eighteen. "They were missionaries, my parents. Spent most of their time in eastern Australia in the blasting desert. Me the only child. My father kicked me out. Haven't spoken to him since."

She wiped at her tears with the back of her right hand and spoke steadily, and my heart sort of broke for her. Until then I'd thought she was English and probably entitled. "It's something I've had to make peace with. Justice told me to come here because he said it would help."

The blond boy, Toby, stood and took the stone from her and talked about wanting to quit smoking while he was in Shashan and how fucking hard it was. He smiled at Maeve the whole time and made her laugh, and in this way you could tell he helped her.

When Toby sat down, the other boy in the kang, Adrian, stood and said, "I am so bad at yoga that none of you better watch. Look away if you see me doing yoga. Save yourselves. I've come for Maeve. Toby and I both have." He didn't seem dramatic about this, and he stared at Justice while he talked, because Justice had this pull over people and I think he got them to be honest.

Hunter stood last and talked about his plane ride to a small landing strip near Shashan on the private jet of a friend who was very senior at Pepsi in China. Maybe Hunter was nervous, but it felt like he bragged about the plane. He had thinning hair swept back from his face, and wore Patagonia or North Face and was one of the American men in China who became more confident the longer they stayed in the country.

"I do this a lot since I got here six months ago." His face looked pinched now, and nervous. "Pick random towns in China to spend the weekend in. But I've never done anything close to this before, and I'm not sure how I even got here. I mean, by plane, yes. But it was some friend of a friend at a cocktail party in the city who put me up to this."

He had a quiet detachment. Almost aloof, and then he changed before our eyes. "Jesus," he said. "Okay, what the hell. My father sent me here. Not here to the mountains, but to China, to run his business. He is large, my father." He laughed and didn't make eye contact with anyone in the circle, so it appeared he was talking to the door. "Not physically large, but punishing. And yes, you could say cruel. Which is probably why the woman at the party thought I should come here." He put the stone back then and sat down, and I didn't know what to believe.

I dreaded the week ahead, because I could see how real intimacy would be required, and I didn't think I was capable of it. It wasn't like I told myself this in an interior monologue. I didn't tell myself anything while I was in Shashan. I reacted. What I think now is that sickness does strange, little invisible things to our minds we can't see.

We stood up from our mats in the yoga house when the Talking Circle was over, and I hoped Shashan would be done soon. I hoped I'd be fixed and back home with Lukas and the girls, but it was still only Friday.

17

About a month before I left for Shashan, Lukas had found me in the basement of Tower Three on my way to get more Belgian beer at the convenience store there. It was surprising to me that they imported beer all the way from Belgium, but the Chinese import many crazy things, like free-range chickens from Ireland and saffron from Egypt and silk nylons from England. Lukas was meant to be putting on yet another private concert for a young Chinese banker, but it had ended early.

"Els," he said when he saw me, and he seemed so worried. "What's wrong? Where are the girls?"

I was not as responsive as I might have been because I'd been drinking, and I was very focused on it—the need for more beer. The bottles were a sophisticated dark brown with a lovely red, Belgian label, and I knew the girls wouldn't wake up. They never woke up.

"The girls," I said, "are asleep. I wanted to get eggs for breakfast." I may have been slurring my words, and I knew that he knew I was lying.

"What if Myla wakes up and you're not there?" He tried

to compose his face, but I'd seen the flash of anger after the worry, which then changed into fear. He was now a little afraid of me and of what I might do next, and this was new in our marriage—the idea that neither of us understood what I was capable of.

"Elisabeth will take care of Myla," I said, which wasn't true, and certainly wasn't fair—to make the younger one be in charge of the older.

"Don't you think that's a lot to ask of a seven-year-old?" Lukas's face was very serious.

I moved by him as if to open the store's glass door with the leather strand of tiny silver bells on it. I thought he would continue home without me. I needed to get the beer. I hadn't considered how I would hide it when I returned, but I wanted it, and this is as embarrassing to me now as anything is from this time, and there's a lot.

Lukas swung his black backpack up onto his back and took my hand firmly in his. "Let's just hope no one has woken up."

I didn't have time to argue, and he didn't say anything else after that and didn't confront me. I knew I would go back the next night when he was out and get the beer. I'd created these small games in my mind. When I would drink. When I would not. When I would get more beer. They were all tests that I guess, in the end, I failed repeatedly, but I kept making up more tests. I would not drink on Tuesdays and Thursdays. But then I would feel very tired on Tuesday, so I'd make an exception because a drink would, for example, help me when I needed to clean up the kitchen after the girls had gone to sleep.

18

On the way out of the yoga house I asked Mei if we could do the Talking Circle drunk the next time. I don't know why I said this. I was joking but not joking, because I didn't know if I'd be able to keep my promise to myself not to drink. You might think this would have been clear. I had two small girls. I would stop drinking. I know this is what Lukas thought. But drinking doesn't work like that, and my need for it was stronger than I realized.

"I cannot perform that task sober again," I said while we stood outside the yoga house in the moonlight. We hardly saw the moon in Beijing because of the smog and the lit-up skyscrapers and the neon signs. "It's not possible to do it sober. So please don't make me." I pretended to be cavalier and as if I was in control of the drinking and not the drinking in control of me.

Mei looked at me. "It will be difficult," she said, "to do the hand standing if you are being drunk." Her English was good but not flawless. "Maybe it is possible," she said and smiled, "that your friend Tasmin can teach you." I was surprised by her sarcasm and how quickly she'd understood Tasmin, and I loved Mei for saying what she'd said.

Then Ulla announced that she and Tasmin and Tamar were walking up to the Lius' house to go to bed. She asked me to leave with them, but I chose to go to the Great Wall instead, and hoped my choice made a small statement about how I wasn't who she thought I was.

The rest of the group followed Justice for twenty minutes to a section of the wall on the ridge to the right of the Lius' house if you looked up from the road, and the sky was navy blue. We don't get that kind of wide sky in Maine. We get stars and the dark navy but not the expansiveness you get in China. A small pile of rocks sat underneath a falling-down part of the wall, and we climbed up here and sat down. Tree brought out a bottle of red wine from her backpack and passed it, and I didn't drink when the bottle came to me. Because of this I honestly thought I'd fixed my drinking problem, which was a sign of my unmooring and maybe also a sign that I hadn't gotten a handle on my thyroid, which I'd found like an enlarged butterfly while fastening beads around my neck before Myla's school Christmas concert.

Justice asked Tree how long she'd been in India, and Tree leaned her head against the side of the wall. "I walked in the northern region near Nepal all winter. It became harder and harder to get away from people, so I walked farther into the mountains until I was as far from others as I could be."

I couldn't imagine being without people entirely, because even though I don't like crowds, to be without people would be to be without the girls and Lukas, which would be the most terrible thing. Mei lit a Yuxi and passed it to me, and I shook my head and gave it back. We all stood along the edge of the wall where the rocks had mostly fallen away, and I looked up at the sky—paler now that the stars were out. I need to say something about how it felt on the wall, because I sensed animals—Chinese wolves and bear—and for a few minutes I was scared but knew I was in the right place. The mountains were outlined in ink as far as I could see into the darkness, and I felt alone, and this was not a bad thing. I almost never experienced being alone because of the girls and Lukas, and I hadn't realized how much territory they took up in my brain. I wasn't sure who I was without them or how this had happened without my noticing it.

China was in my blood then, the way Tree had earlier said it was in her blood, even though when she'd said it she'd seemed a little ridiculous. What I mean is that China felt important on that wall, like the most important place in the world. I never smoked pot after the children, but I had the feeling of being outside my body on the Great Wall, and I loved this feeling when I was stoned in high school. It was close to the feeling I got when my painting went well.

"You have cancer of the arm, Elsey?" Mei asked me.

I was surprised again that she was so direct, and I appreciated it. I thought to tell her about the zinging pain in my elbow and how it scared me, because what was it? But I didn't want to burden her with it. I hardly knew her, even though I felt like I knew her. "No," I said. "No arm cancer."

She took a last drag of her cigarette and rubbed it on the sole of her sandal. "It was the truth wrapped in a lie."

"Yes, that's it. But I feel bad about it."

"We do not need to know your secrets here. Keep them safe in China."

I saw that she didn't operate out of guilt, and I was envious of this, too. I couldn't keep track of the different people in my life that I was in the act of letting down. She asked me if I liked the Great Wall, and I said yes, very much.

I rarely talked to any of the Chinese like this. I mean, Ulla had Chinese colleagues who came to her larger dinner parties, and I chatted with them, but it seemed formal and not like talking to Mei. Her fame also aroused my curiosity, so there was a little bit of that, too. I can't lie. She told me she was trying to understand foreigners like me who projected things onto the Wall and made the wall into something bigger than it was until it wasn't a wall anymore but a distorted symbol of China. "You must forgive me for criticizing you."

I didn't feel she was criticizing me. "I'm not offended," I said, and vowed to give the Wall more thought when the pain in my arm had subsided.

"I had a husband once," Tree said and took another sip from the bottle, and I could see some of her teeth in the dark. Her hair had curled a lot more in the mist and rose around her face like a little hive. "He fell out of love with me when I had no money and worked in a fruit processing plant in Auckland. He let me have the couch, and he took the bed. He didn't worry about me. He never worried about me."

Andre said he was glad he was single now. "It's too difficult to work for the airline and have the love life." He exhaled loudly and reached for the bottle and took a big sip and passed the bottle to Maeve, who drank and passed it to Toby. Toby pushed his glasses higher on his nose and drank and passed the bottle to Adrian, who drank and handed it to Justice, who to my relief put the bottle by his feet.

I thought how Lukas slept without any clothes on and ran naked down the hall in the morning to make the coffee. I knew Lukas would never stop running down the hall naked in the morning, and that there were things to fight in a marriage and things to let go of. I thought also of how Lukas was the Chinese bear in winter that I wrapped my arms around in bed to keep warm. And how he worried for me during the surgery and brought my favorite steamed buns with red-bean paste to the hospital as a surprise.

· 19 ·

During my first month in Beijing, we'd wake up in the dark and reach for each other and I felt almost crazed with it, and it went on like this for quite some time. He came home one night wearing a black flight suit with a zipper down the front. We'd probably been married three weeks, and it was two in the morning, and I walked into the kitchen to get water. He was at the sink filling a glass, a little unreachable after his time in the club. This was the old apartment with the view of the back of the Workers Stadium and the formica kitchen and the pink plastic rice cooker. I'd been painting and drinking scotch, and I wanted to remove the flight suit and press into him and absorb him, and I did this.

My paintings were still my children, and the metaphor is obvious but I need to say it because I cared for the pieces like they were a part of me. The paintings were no longer about whether the women were beautiful anymore, which was important in the context of my career. I very much wanted a career. These paintings looked like mistakes—lemon yellows and lawn greens and marines. The women's stories were underneath and that was enough, and the work sold at higher and higher prices.

It sold to expats in China because of my art dealer, a Finnish woman named Bree who wore ropes of gold and was married to second-in-command at Apple in China. She had a deep network and was able to get my paintings to the Europeans. This was my more important market. I'd had shows by then in London and Prague and Paris. After Saatchi began representing me, buyers paid $25,000 and waited on me to finish commissions. All this happened over many years and feels to me almost like a dream, because painting was my life then.

I gave birth to Myla four years after I moved to Beijing and Elisabeth eleven months later. I don't know how to explain this, except that everything in my life changed after I had children. I didn't understand how to parent. No one really knows how to parent until they have kids, but I've often worried that I parent scared, because this was how I took care of my sisters in our house in the woods. I thought I could save them if bad men came for us while our parents were gone. I didn't know there were ways to protect the people you loved and not be fearful. Or that we don't control very much of anything that happens anyway.

The girls were one and two and then three and four. I learned to cook the things my children would eat. I still tried to paint. I felt guilty when I painted and wasn't with the girls, but I was unsettled when I was with the girls and didn't paint. I kept a secret log of my hours painting and my hours with the girls, and I spent parts of the day adding up the hours in my head so they would be equal. It was my sickness in a way. Not to be in the painting when I was painting, and not to be with the girls when I was with the girls.

I liked to be alone when I painted. There was no other way to do it. Painting was an evisceration of any lies I told myself. When Myla was five, I told her she was stupid for not taking a nap, and this may be the hardest thing to write. I wanted her to nap very badly so I could paint. I was still consumed by the paintings, and I threw a blanket at Myla that landed partly on her head in her bed, and she began to cry. For weeks afterward she said, "Am I still stupid, Mama? Am I stupid today?"

Sometimes the painting went well in my studio in an old war factory in Dashanzi thirty minutes from our apartment. Sometimes the days with the girls were quiet and uneventful, and I was the luckiest person to know my children. But these days were rare, and the painting was like a compulsion. It was the only thing I'd done well, and I couldn't look at my life or ask myself if I needed to be doing the things I was doing anymore.

When Myla started school near the new shopping mall in Sanlitun, I went to my first parents' association meeting there, led by a child psychologist mother from Singapore who asked us each to say one thing we thought we were good at as parents.

I didn't believe there was one. It seemed like a trance had taken hold of expat mothers I knew in Beijing: Cloth diapers shipped from England. Organic pears from France. Online math programs for our three-year-olds. I didn't judge them for this as much as try to keep up, and I couldn't keep up and experienced a quiet sense of unrest no one could see. Not my husband. It was invisible and was everything to me, this unrest. The time in my life when I painted was ending. I could feel it ending. It had begun to seem luxurious—hours alone painting, and this was my downfall, when I made it something that created a debt against my girls.

At the parents' meeting, I was still trying to hold on to ideas I could paint—things about what it meant to live in a woman's body, and how the body got manipulated by the representation of it. I held these ideas in a small corner of my mind and tried to bring them out when I was alone in my studio, until it got to the point where this no longer worked and the ideas seemed foreign and honestly sort of odd, and I stopped going to the studio and stopped painting.

When my turn to talk at the meeting came, I said, "What about affection?" It was my only thought—that I often hugged my girls. "Does that count?"

A Chinese woman next to me in a lime green Hermès scarf nodded. There were other immaculately dressed mothers there from South Korea and India and Bahrain and Russia, but the Chinese woman spoke first. "I had not previously considered affection as a parenting trait."

I felt embarrassed. But the woman smiled at me and wrote down what I'd said on her iPhone—I could see it on her List of Things to Do as a Parent. Hug the Children More.

"If you fucking push me, I'll find you in your sleep," Maeve
said to Toby and Adrian. They'd grabbed her by the shoulders
and for a moment seemed about to send her over the side.
Then they let her go, and we all stood on the wall looking
down at the ground. It seemed far to jump, so I turned and
used the wall like a ladder, and Mei came next, and I held
her elbow and her shoulder. Tree tried going face-forward,
inching her way, but she slipped and landed badly on the
rocks. I remember it was hard to see, because low clouds had
blocked the moon. Justice jumped down after her and made
Tree straighten out her leg. She needed help walking, and
Justice carried her on his back. She rested her head on his
neck and closed her eyes and looked like a sleepy child, and
I had to pee quite badly so I followed them because I wasn't
sure how to get to the Lius' on my own.

Their house sat underneath the first big curve of the
mountain, but for a while I had no idea of distance or where
the house was in relation, and I studied my feet in the dark

so I didn't fall. Mei and Andre and Hunter were somewhere behind me, and the three kang sleepers behind them. The sensation of being on the mountain in the dark without my girls was the same reckless feeling I'd had earlier on the wall. I will say that I thought I was in control when I drank at home alone, but I see now that I was also reckless. This sounds confusing. The drinking was the one thing I thought I controlled. How many drinks. One or two or three. I didn't see the consequences. I didn't know, for example, how my drinking hurt other people. I didn't understand that when I drank, my husband could still see me and that my oblivion didn't work both ways.

I hurried to keep up with Justice. What was I doing with strangers instead of home with the girls? I won't say being in Shashan was a punishment, though there was some of that. Mostly it was disorienting to be alone on the mountain at night, and I wanted to call Lukas and tell him about it, but I remembered he might not want to hear from me and that I was walking in the dark back to the Lius' house because I was weak and couldn't stop drinking. I worked hard then to remember Lukas loved me and my girls loved me and that I wasn't being punished. I was being helped.

I stayed caught between being weak and being helped, and in this way Shashan called on me to clarify something about myself. Did I love myself or hate myself? Until I met Lukas I didn't know there were people who liked themselves even with the damage they carried. People for whom life was maybe simpler and who had never considered hating

themselves. He was one of them. He liked to ask me questions, and in this way he was different from men I've known.
How are you feeling? Do you have a fever? Can I make you
tea? Can I tell the nurse with the bad attitude to get the
fuck out of your hospital room? Can I make rice? I didn't
often answer him, and I see now that he was trying to let me
know he saw me for who I was. But he was also trying to fix
things, and it has taken me time to understand that my quiet
didn't mean I had deficiencies he needed to compensate for.

22

Lukas's father received a degree in engineering at the University of Copenhagen in 1973, but he didn't find work in the engineering firms in the capital, so instead he became a sought-after train mechanic. When Lukas was five, his father drove him to a youth soccer academy on the east side of the capital for a tryout, and the directors of the academy told his father that his son was too young to try out, but his father insisted that his son be allowed to participate anyway. He was a loud man when he wanted to be and he achieved, Lukas has told me, a way of communicating through syllabic grunting.

It's hard to get Lukas to talk about his father, and what I've assembled has been extracted over years, but what I know about the academy's soccer fields is that they're back behind the train station on the east side, and that this was how Lukas's father got the idea—by spending each day underneath the bowel of a train, watching the boys in the soccer academy kick balls.

On the drive to the tryout he'd told Lukas that the life

he wanted for his son was the life of soccer, not the life of a mechanic on the track in the fucking sun. Lukas told me that he played fine in the soccer tryout, but he was a five-year-old among ten-year-olds and that on the day of the academy tryout he was smaller by two hands than most of the boys, so he couldn't get to some of the balls passed to the wing where the academy directors put him so he wouldn't get hurt in the middle. You need to be fast on the wing, Lukas explained to me. And he was fast, but also small back then, and it was inevitable he missed balls.

His father cuffed him on the head when they got in the car after the tryout and then again once they'd started driving and said it was for missing balls passed to the wing. Then his father couldn't contain himself it seems and pulled over to the side of the road and beat Lukas with his fists. Neither he nor his father spoke of the tryout or the beating to Lukas's mother when they got home. She was a cello player in the city orchestra and a practicing Christian and was often distracted by her busy schedule and by trying to cook meals for Lukas's father.

It's only recently that Lukas explained to me the small room in the back of their house with the black-and-white television and the empty bottles lined up on the floor by his father's wool chair. And how his father would call him into this room with the cigarettes and vodka to watch a replay of a particular soccer goal and then cuff Lukas on the ear or wherever he could reach from his chair for not being a better soccer player.

His father made Lukas try out for the soccer academy every year, and every year the academy directors had a different reason for why Lukas wasn't admitted. He was a good soccer player; Lukas has made this clear to me. He thinks his father made the directors uncomfortable with his syllabic way of speaking that was often like grunting and his forcefulness, and that the academy directors wanted to make his father go away.

"You could tell as soon as we got out of the car," Lukas told me once. "To admit me into the academy was to make a relationship with my father and the directors weren't willing to do that." He knew this after the second year, which made the tryouts more painful because he said he could have made it, and I take him at his word. He ended up turning to music and away from soccer and away from his father in a definitive way.

23

The whole time we walked down the mountain I was afraid
I'd lose Justice and Tree and be left alone with the Chinese
bears. We turned the last corner on the path, and I thought
I could see the kerosene lamps on the terrace. When we got
to the terrace, I stood on the side in the dark and waited for
Mei and the others. Justice sat Tree down at the table and
got gauze in his room and taped it over the cut she'd gotten
on the sole of her foot. Then the two of them went to their
rooms.

The kang sleepers laughed and tiptoed into the Lius'
house, and Andre said he was exhausted and waved good
night. Mei and Hunter were the last, and Hunter smiled at
me distractedly and went to his room, but Mei and I stood
for a moment and watched the cats circle the eel cistern on
the far side of the terrace. Then a man stepped out of the
darkness and called her name. Leng was probably, after Ai
Weiwei, the most famous artist in China, and he wore the
workers' blue chamois pants and matching jacket. His head

was squarish like the top of a wooden mallet, and he smiled at Mei, but she didn't acknowledge at first that she knew him.

He stepped closer, and she didn't move back. He took another step. She closed her eyes. I decided that he'd come to apologize, and this hope made me think of what my own marriage was lacking, and instead of turning away from my marriage like I had since I'd gotten sick, I wanted to drive home and fix it.

Leng tossed his cigarette on the terrace and put his hands on his hips and looked at his wife for another thirty seconds. Maybe it was a full minute. She still had her eyes closed. They stood less than one foot apart. Then he took her wrist. I've become pretty fluent in Mandarin, even though I don't think I'll ever understand the slang, but what Leng said to Mei was easy because it was repetitive. He said he wanted her to go home with him.

That phrasing—"Come home with me." Maybe three times. I watched her face, and it didn't change. Closed and in pain. Then she moved her head to the side almost imperceptibly. He stepped in a few inches and took both her hands and placed them behind her, and she let him do this. His body blocked my view, so I couldn't tell what she did with her face, but the position looked uncomfortable, and I worried about her and tried to solve for where we were in the order of the universe. What I mean is I couldn't understand how I'd come to be with Leng and Mei on the mountain, so I was trying to give it bigger meaning. I do this—give things bigger meaning than they deserve—and it can be a mistake.

I also rooted for Leng and Mei on the terrace the way I root for my own marriage, and I don't know exactly what I'm rooting for, but it's a sentiment that feels important. I was now somehow involved in Mei's life. We hadn't made claims on each other, but it seemed understood that I'd wait on the terrace. Leng took her right arm in both hands and tried to pull her down toward the parking area, and she cried in a deeper voice than I thought she had, and I looked up at the sky and wanted to be standing anywhere but on that terrace.

He said something sharper and pulled on her arm so her whole body shook, and this didn't look like affection. She was able to move away from him, and he talked softly to her again and stepped toward her with his arms out to the sides the way I've seen people do when they're trying to corner birds. Mrs. Liu kept chickens, and Toby had tried to catch one on the terrace after dinner, but the chicken got away and I was relieved, because what was he going to do with the bird if he got it?

Leng said something I couldn't understand, but I could tell he was angry. I heard Hunter's door open, and he came out of his room, which was next to Mei's room. He was taller than Leng and overall much bigger, and he asked Mei if she was okay, and she said yes and that he could go back to sleep. He didn't, though. And this was the right thing to do at the time. To stand there.

It was probably close to eleven o'clock at night, and the village was almost completely quiet. The dogs and donkeys and chickens slept. Things changed after Hunter came outside.

Leng didn't try to touch Mei again. She had her hand on the doorknob of her room. But then she put her arms around Leng, and they stood together for a long while forehead-to-forehead, which was surprising. I could tell she was crying by the way her shoulders shook. Then she stepped back and stared at him and waited.

Before he left, he said loudly that he didn't like the American sleeping in the room next door to her, and that he would kill the American if he learned this man had touched his wife. Then he turned and walked across the terrace past me, though I don't think he saw me. I also don't think Hunter understood anything Leng said, because he waved at Mei and told her to have a good night and went back in his room, and Mei opened her door and stepped inside.

I wouldn't have guessed at the sadness in Mei's life, but there's a lot we don't know. I didn't know the man named Hunter, for example, but we were both now somehow charged with keeping Mei safe. No one said it, and she didn't ask, but it felt that way. This happens—that I'm allied with people who are unaware I'm allied with them.

My room had a broken TV on a laminate bureau pushed up against the wall, and I lay down on the bed with the nylon bedspread and thought about the configuration of Myla and Elisabeth's beds in our apartment. They've lived there since they were born. I tried to see their faces, and I could hold them in my mind until they almost looked real, but then their hair and faces were gone and wouldn't appear fully formed. The girls spent most of their time in the apartment in Elisabeth's room, because it was bigger and had a rope swing Lukas had hung from the ceiling and a wall covered with paper so the girls could draw, but mostly Elisabeth kicked balls in there.

You could also watch the hutong out the enormous window. It had about eighty one-story houses like barracks, and for years the girls and I wondered whether or not the hutong would be torn down and replaced with high-rises. Lukas also worried about this, but it wasn't one of his chief worries, so he didn't watch the comings and goings of the people the way the girls and I did. Every month or so we heard something different: The hutong was going. The hutong was staying. We watched for bulldozers out the window and rooted for the hutong as if we understood something essential about China's past when we knew nothing. For a long time the girls and I wanted Lukas to root for it, too, and we told him he wasn't paying enough attention to it. He was caught up in his music, and I wonder now if we thought he wasn't paying enough attention to us, but I think he was. I just wasn't able to see it.

On Saturday morning we ate rice porridge on the terrace, and it's hard to explain how beautiful the valley looked from up there and how loud the absence of construction equipment was. The sun was full and made the clouds seem whiter and closer to the mountain. Sometimes I'm amazed at the scope, and I've told my sister Ginny several times that she needs to come to China and understand for herself. I often think if you haven't been to China, you can't really talk about the state of the world, but Ginny hasn't come yet.

We walked down to the yoga house after the porridge, and I didn't speak with Mei about what I'd seen the night before. There wasn't time to talk. At breakfast I'd heard that Tamar had left before dawn, and we were quieter while we walked, silent almost, and her absence opened up the real possibility of going home. The village also seemed silent. I understand now that most children had been sent to military boarding schools, and others had left Shashan with their parents to look for work in the cities because there was no work left in the village. In this way the village felt emptied except for the old women in blazers who were like ghosts, and a few families like the Lius testing the tourist business.

I set up my mat in the back of the house and bent at my waist and tried to touch my hands to the ground, and I saw the Hong Kong hospital where I had my small operation. In Beijing if you have money, you can get medical information quickly, and there are no waits or protocols. You receive X-rays and ultrasounds not long after you arrive at the doctor's office. In the end we were sent to Hong Kong. But we had no parents we could bring with us, so it didn't seem like a solution at first, because who would watch the children?

My sister Ginny came to Hong Kong, and I'll never forget that. She had her own family in San Francisco and had become the type of evangelical Christian with no birthdays or singing, and I was certain it was Jehovah's Witnesses, though I tried not to ask. She met her husband through a financial literacy program for soldiers that she ran at the local bank, and neither of them voted because they said what happened on earth wasn't what mattered.

Tommy Miller, the neurosurgeon I'd lived with in Dublin, had a medical practice in Hong Kong, and I'd learned this from a painter friend in Ireland who was still in touch with both of us. Tommy didn't work at the hospital where I was going, but I thought he could help me and I wrote him and asked him for lunch the day before my surgery. We met at the American Club, where he was a member, and the dining room had big potted palm trees and white linen and checkerboard yellow sisal, and it felt calm in there and orderly. He chose the tenderloin for both of us, and I don't know why I let him order for me, but I felt young again like we were back in Dublin. After I'd left him and moved in with the owners of the Montessori school, he gave me the chance to go back to him and I almost did. I was selling my paintings by then—the earlier, more literal interpretations in the exaggerated David Hockney colors. But in the end I didn't go back, because he wanted to marry me and said he'd wait as long as it took.

Ginny hadn't arrived in Hong Kong yet from California, and Lukas had taken the girls on the ferry to Kowloon because they loved boats and he needed something to do with them. Were they okay on the ferry? Had Lukas gotten them enough food? When the waiter came back with the iced teas, I ordered a dirty martini, and Tommy said, "You are so thin. You look wonderful." I wanted to tell him, "I have always been this thin."

I have a writer friend in Beijing now who says when we see people, we see with desire. Which means we see what we want to see. I think there's truth in this. Maybe Tommy saw my thinness as if he'd never seen it before, because he wanted to see it. I think at first he thought I was finally returning to him, because why else had I found him in Hong Kong? He was seeing what he wanted to see. I remembered why I'd left him then, and I wanted to leave him again and stand and walk out of the American Club. But after he said I looked thin, I thanked him and stayed in the awkwardness and didn't try to get out of it. I still wanted something from him. But I was glad for my own marriage and felt a small joy for Lukas. Joy for the ferry to Kowloon and the girls.

"If you want to smoke pot in Hong Kong, Elsey," Tommy said, "you must do it in your room and don't ever leave your rolling papers out or the cleaning staff will report you to the police and you'll be put in prison."

Had he always talked to me like a child? My hair was long and curlier in the humidity, and I was wearing a favorite Japanese sundress with a blue tie-dye pattern. Maybe I wore the tie-dye to provoke Tommy, because I wanted him to know I was different than I'd been in Dublin and had turned out better than I would have if I'd married him. More creative. Someone who wore tie-dye. This was the only word I could think of while I sat in the American Club and listened to him. That he wasn't creative and I was. I was ridiculous. I don't even know if it's true that Tommy isn't creative. He's a good man.

"Don't get caught by the police with drugs in Hong Kong," he said, and I could see he was still mad at me for not choosing him. He wore a pink bow tie and had the bluest eyes and had become sensible in Hong Kong, and he wasn't this way in Dublin yet. He was still a little reckless, but maybe it was a controlled recklessness. I think I left him because he was in love with me and I didn't like myself enough. After he'd given me my first cocaine at a U2 concert in Belfast, I remember feeling euphoric, but also clear that I'd leave him. It was much easier to leave. I mean that. To stay with Lukas has been harder than leaving him.

"I have children now," I told Tommy after the cold soup

was placed on the table. "Two girls. I don't have time or inclination to smoke pot."

I saw my marriage as separate from Tommy Miller and the American Club. I knew even then that it was my own fault I'd stopped painting. I couldn't blame my marriage. I'd thought my girls needed me more than they did, and I tried to let this define me—their need. I thought it was my duty until it had begun to feel like a small pathology. But I couldn't stop, and I had fixed ideas of who my girls were, which weren't entirely accurate.

I drank my martini and got high on it and was also angry with Tommy Miller for assuming I was doing drugs. What did I want from him? I wanted a better excuse for leaving him in Dublin. I'll admit that I also wanted help from his colleagues at the hospital and for him to feel bad for me so that his compassion erased any negative feelings he'd had for me in Ireland, and this was exactly what happened.

25

In Ireland, Tommy Miller and I once drove over something high and dramatic and terrifying called the Conor Pass, which was at ten thousand feet and had a one-lane road and a steep green hedge on either side and pastures and stone walls. Tommy drove and I held my breath and watched the mountains and the round-horned sheep, and the past felt very close the way it also does in China. But in Ireland the story seemed clearer: Here were the stone gates. Here was the paddock and the startling hedge. Here was your life.

We came down out of the mountains and stopped at a beach shaped like a long kitchen utensil, and I felt so alive. We got out of the car and looked across the churning sea, and in my mind I could see my parents in their brick house in America. The particularity of my mother's sadness had been scary after Margaret died, and I couldn't look at it directly. It had gotten so that her sadness blocked out my sadness until I didn't know what I felt. I stood on the beach in Ireland and asked my parents how they were coping without her. Without Margaret. "This is how I'm coping," I said to myself. By not coming home.

Tommy and I slept in a renovated stable a few miles from the beach that had an earth roof with grass growing out of it. There was a yellow crushed-velvet couch and a metal stove and peat moss. The front door was glass and opened to a yard where wrens landed, and I left the door open when we got there, and one of the wrens flew inside. I was afraid it would panic and bang into the walls, and I tried showing it how to go back outside, but the bird stood on the wooden floor near the couch and studied my face.

I think of it as the only time my sister has come back for me, and I am not a superstitious person. Margaret wasn't the bird exactly, but she was at the same time an approximation of the bird, and I wanted to tell this to Tommy when he came into the living room with wet hair after his shower. I was still feeling the aliveness from the beach and the terrifying drive, and I was so happy about the bird I almost cannot say. Then Tommy shooed the bird out of the house very quickly before I had time to stop him, and I couldn't believe what he'd done but I didn't tell him.

26

The hospital sat on a small hill in the north part of Hong Kong where there were more palm trees and it felt for minutes at a time in the cab like we were in rural Hawaii. It was a new, concrete hospital with many small square glass windows in a row. The waiting room outside the surgery unit had silky carpet and a snack cart with plastic carafes of Starbucks coffee. I felt alone in this waiting room. Lukas wanted to talk about how I was feeling and he took my hand, and I wasn't able to talk back to him. I appeared to be in the waiting room with him, but I was defensed.

This was the word the man I pay in Beijing to ask me questions used, and I don't like this word, but it's true, I was defensed in the hospital. There were many times when my sister Margaret had to have injections, and before they began to get her arms ready to receive the shots, she'd close her eyes and become removed from us.

I tried to erase myself from my husband and the food cart and the real estate magazines. I'd become willful by then and needed to control the story. In this way I thought I was protecting my children. I think I was also trying to protect myself. I thought if you erased yourself from the story you didn't feel the pain.

The day after my surgery, my Chinese surgeon came to my hospital room to check on me, and I said I was so worried about my children, who were alone with my sister at the hotel. I could hardly catch my breath, I talked so fast to him. My surgeon was young—maybe thirty—with rectangular, stainless steel glasses and a professional distance I'd found unnerving. But now he looked at me kindly and told me not to worry. He said when a child wakes up in the morning, he often runs through a safety checklist in his mind.

"A girl, for example," my surgeon said, "will ask herself, 'Am I safe this morning in this bed? Is there anything that is going to hurt me?'"

I was surprised my surgeon knew these things. They were important things, and I listened intently. I saw my surgeon differently, and that he was more perceptive and understanding than I'd thought, and it's amazing how much it mattered that I felt better about him.

"The child isn't aware that he's running through this checklist," he said. "The checklist is really something more primal than deliberate or conscious. I can guarantee to you, Elsey, that your two girls know they are safe."

My guess is that during the time I was in the hospital and my girls were in the hotel in Hong Kong without me, they went through their checklists in the morning and didn't feel as safe as they usually did. I mean, where was I? Where was their mother? Attached to tubes and monitors in a hospital that resembled a cruise ship on a hill in Hong Kong.

It got so I had to put the girls out of my mind, which is what Lukas still accuses me of doing to the people I love. I think the girls understood in theory that Ginny was my sister—but they didn't really know her. She was loving to them and bought them gelato in Hong Kong, but she wasn't their mother. Still, it was okay. I keep reminding myself even now that it was okay.

The girls hardly asked about my surgery when I got back to the hotel, and this was where Ginny and Lukas had more work to do because the girls wanted to cuddle with me in bed. Ginny had brown hair tucked behind her ears then, and defined leg muscles because she ran a lot. If there was ever a crisis, she was efficient in a way I was not, though I've never been sure what she's hiding. She and Lukas took the girls on the ferry again and for haircuts so I could sleep, but the girls got tired and wanted to come back to the hotel room and see me.

I was meant to be very still, and I didn't sleep. I don't think Lukas slept, either. The hotel room looked like a formal town house in Charleston, South Carolina, where a man and his wife who'd bought two of my paintings once flew me from Ireland. They had a reception for me in their house with chintz upholstery and ceramic poodle doorstops. I have to think that this couple bought my paintings to be closer to the original paintings I reinterpreted, because some people like this feeling of prestige that the original gives them, but I can't be sure.

We had a suite, and the girls had beds in a room with a green linen couch, and there was another double bed in the far-right corner of this room for Ginny. Everything in the hotel was palm trees and lime greens and teak. The girls thought it was fancy. We got room service with glass bottles of Coke for them, and they haven't forgotten this. They still talk about this time as if we were on vacation, and in some ways we were. The room Lukas and I slept in also served as the main living room, and there was a small seating area with cushioned rattan chairs and the chintz couch and a galley kitchen with a stainless fridge. Lukas and I grew very close in some ways here, and I think of this hotel fondly sometimes. Because of the way he held my hand at night.

But it was also the beginning of the time when I became more closed off, and he couldn't reach me. It didn't seem significant at first. But I didn't tell him how my small surgery had taken me to the time of Margaret's surgeries, though it's obvious now.

I've thought of telling the girls how scared I was in Hong Kong, but I see now that you don't get to make that kind of confession to your kids. Or I don't. They're still kids. Maybe when Myla is fifty and I'm eighty I'll tell her how scared I was in Hong Kong, but then it will seem overly dramatic because I'll still be alive.

27

We walked to the yoga house after breakfast on Saturday, and Justice demonstrated the Sun Salutation again by putting his arms up to the ceiling, then bending at his waist and stretching his arms out like a platform diver. Then he lowered his body and came back to standing. Arms in the air again. Child's Pose meant essentially kneeling with your face down on your mat, and it was the pose Justice said we should do if we felt too tired to do the other poses. Several people in the yoga house must have been tired that morning, because they all had their faces down on their mats—Maeve and Toby and Adrian and Mei. Hunter did extra Sun Salutations, and Andre sat with his eyes closed in some kind of meditation and didn't follow any of Justice's instructions.

After lunch we were given what Justice called personal time. We could stay in our rooms or walk the goat paths around the mountain. I didn't want to walk with anyone else, but I also didn't want to get lost, so I stayed in my room. It was the first time in years I didn't have a computer or a phone or a television that worked. I looked through the gaps in the plastic blinds, and the sky was chalk with a layer of milk blue underneath, and I didn't do anything with this color—I didn't get out a sketchbook, because I hadn't brought one. But I saw how I could paint the sky, and I hadn't seen that in years. Then one of the village dogs barked, and I got up from the bed to pee. When I lay back down, the color of the sky had changed.

28

The second Talking Circle was Saturday night after the yoga, and Tasmin told us her husband was sleeping with a young Chinese opera star in Zhenjiang. I knew her husband kept an apartment in Zhenjiang, and I'd heard rumors about Chinese singers, so what Tasmin said didn't surprise me exactly. What surprised me was that she'd told us about it. I could see she was hurt and maybe had always been hurt by her husband and was showing it.

This was a different version of Tasmin than she promoted in the city, and it's one of the things we can't know—which version a person is. But I think sooner or later the truth comes out if you're on a small mountain north of Huairou doing yoga in a house with no floor. I'm not sure she'd planned to tell us her secret, and I don't know if she regretted it afterward, but I was glad she told us, because I hadn't known she was hurting. Of course she hurt.

After Tasmin sat down, Ulla took the stone. "I am looking," she said, "for evidence of a rare Mongolian hawk rumored to still live in these mountains." She nodded to herself and looked over at Justice. "My hope is to have one proper sighting to report. There will be variegated purple plumage on the bird's breastbone. Please come find me if you think you see one."

Tasmin had taken a risk talking about the opera star, and she was hurting, and I thought we should all somehow acknowledge it. Maybe the hawk was Ulla's way of changing the subject, but it was as if she'd become disconnected from Tasmin and Tasmin's pain and the yoga house and what was going on there. It wasn't hard to do. I, too, wanted to pretend what was happening in the yoga house wasn't happening.

I waited. Tree went next and talked about leaving Auckland and her strong wish to have a child. Then Andre stood and said he'd broken with his lover of two years a few weeks earlier because this man wanted to adopt a baby. "I decided many years ago not to be a parent. Not because of any objection I have, but because I am afraid I am unfit. I am never home." He said it was his destiny not to be a father and that he believed in his destiny, and I don't think any of us took our eyes off him while he spoke. I wanted to ask him what in the world he was talking about because I thought he'd make a wonderful father, but the rule was you couldn't talk back during Talking Circle.

The kang sleepers mostly told jokes about how hard it was to be three to the bed and how Maeve kicked them in her sleep, and they were gentle with one another, and many of us laughed. Everyone seemed less self-conscious, as if they'd realized we were going to be in the mountains for six more days so they could slow down. But the Talking Circle was still excruciating for me.

Hunter took the stone and said he was single at thirty because his father had refused each of the three women Hunter had brought home to marry. "He has been clear that none of them meet his standards, and now I suspect he sent me to China to keep me alone." Hunter said this last part in an exaggerated voice. Like he was overexplaining it on purpose for effect, but he also sounded a little desperate. "I'm beginning to wonder what I'm doing here. In Shashan. Something about this place—these mountains—is making me feel crazy. No concentration. No sleep." Then he laughed and put the stone down and he was done.

It got quiet after that. Mei finally stood. "I am not understanding this tendency to want to fill empty space." She shrugged. "Okay. I keep many wigs at my home and I am becoming different people depending on the wig I am wearing." She laughed. "I am thinking of myself now as a robber."

She looked around the house. "Stealing looks. But it is good here. I am not wearing any wigs and it is my naturalized hair I have today." She put the stone back on the rug and sat.

I went after Mei. There was no one else left. I said I'd been afraid to tell the truth before, but that I didn't have arm cancer. It wasn't as painful as I thought it would be to say this, because the whole process of the Talking Circle was odd and formulaic and effective, and I found myself not caring what people thought. It was a relief. If anything, Justice said we needed to be honest, so at least I was honest. I told them also that I'd been sick for a bit before with my thyroid, and now I was better but sometimes the worry still got to me and my mind played tricks.

We climbed the hill to the Lius' house after that, and maybe we were a little stunned by the Talking Circle and that we were still in Shashan and that the week wasn't even half over. I was self-conscious because I'd shared my secret and couldn't tell if any of the others were able to acknowledge it, or if they thought I was deranged for lying. There are moments like this when I'm away from my girls and time moves incredibly slowly. It crawls.

I pulled the blinds in my room so no light came through. Then I climbed into bed and didn't see my girls' faces or bodies but had a feeling of who they were, and this was calming. There was no art on the walls of my room. Nothing at all to look at. When we were in the Hong Kong hotel Myla drew stick figures of our family with words underneath: "This is my sister with a scrape on her eye. This is my mum. This is my dad. Mum and Dad are holding hands in front of the dragon." I don't know why Ginny wrote the word "Mum." We've never called our mother Mum, only Mom. I think Ginny changed in California and that her own children called her Mum and that's fine. It interested me, this word Mum, because it was more casual than Mom in some ways, but it wasn't what my girls called me. They called me Mama or Mom. I loved the drawing that Myla made, because Lukas and I were holding hands in front of the dragon. That was the painting to me. The fact that we were holding hands said everything would be okay, and I think it will be.

Elisabeth made me a painting in Hong Kong of three neon-pink flowers with green stems, and they're rough but you can tell they're tulips. She had a friend in preschool that year named Lena who was part Vietnamese and part Dutch, and Lena cried every day unless she was making drawings with Elisabeth. Cried and cried. So every day their teacher Mrs. Carter set them up at the low formica table in the corner near the bean-bag chairs, and this is where Elisabeth learned to make the flowers. I think she was sympathetic to Lena and was able to show her that. She drew me something else in Hong Kong called a Gigantic Blowfish with one hundred sections in its stomach, each a different color. I still have these paintings.

29

The first night in the hotel, after the girls went to sleep, I asked Lukas to get out the bottle of white wine in the refrigerator and pour me an enormous glass. I didn't think he or Ginny could say no to anything I asked. Ginny was watching a popular Chinese game show where adult contestants dressed up like young children and sang patriotic school songs, and I lay on the couch staring at the screen.

Lukas brought the glass to me and whispered that I should go slowly. "It's dangerous, you know. I've researched it. To drink on painkillers."

I looked at him like I didn't understand and reached for the wine.

"Don't do this, Elsey," he whispered.

By the third day in Hong Kong I thought I was almost completely fine, and we all rode a bus to the western part of the island and took a metal tram to the top. Vendors sold satay sticks up there and pork buns and apples and gum, and Lukas held both of the girls' hands by the railing on the viewing platform. I think he thought he was helping me by doing this, but I felt far away from the girls and wanted to hold their hands, and it was the beginning of me not feeling needed.

Ginny took the girls to the bathroom, and Lukas and I bought postcards of the skyline and stood looking out at the bay down below, which was as blue as the sky. When the girls came back, they asked to buy the gum, and I said no, and Lukas wavered and looked at me and also said no. On the way down in the tram, I saw Myla was chewing something bright pink, and I asked her where she'd gotten it and she pointed to Elisabeth. I kneeled down in front of Elisabeth in the tram so I was at eye level. "Where did you get the gum, Elisabeth?"

I put out my hand, and she began crying. "The man gave it to us."

"What man?" I looked at Lukas and he shrugged, so I looked at Ginny. She was wearing an oversized straw visor she'd bought on top of the mountain, and she turned so she was facing away from me. Neither of them seemed con- cerned about the gum.

"What man, Myla?" She was in the corner of the tram leaning in to Ginny's legs now, and she started crying, too.

"The man selling the apples." Myla sobbed. "He gave us each a piece."

"And what did Daddy and I say about the gum?" I stared at them both and would not let them look away. "You have let us down."

"But we didn't steal it. We didn't steal it. He gave it to us!" Elisabeth yelled.

"But it was sneaky. And being sneaky is like lying, which is very close to stealing." I can't account fully for what I said to them, but I am making myself put it down here on the page. Elisabeth began to sob and sob, and when we got off, Lukas looked at me for a long second on the sidewalk. We found burgers for the girls, but Elisabeth wouldn't eat hers because she was crying too hard, and she kept saying she wanted to know what the punishment was. I knew if she ate something, she'd stop crying, because I could tell she was really hungry and tired.

"I have to know the punishment!"

"I'm not sure. I need to think about it, but it will involve not swimming in the pool at the hotel." I see now that I was out of my mind when I said this, and that I still wanted some kind of control, and that there's no way to get this time back with my girls.

"I have to know now! I have to know!" Elisabeth said. "I cannot have a normal day until I know and what I want more than anything now is a normal day! So could we have that? Just a normal day, please? Please? Please?"

Lukas stared at me in the burger place. He stared and stared until I stood down. "Yes. We can now have a normal day."

On our last night in Hong Kong, I lay with my feet hanging over the arm of the green couch because it was a small couch, and I had the wineglass on my chest and my hand on the rim of the glass to balance it. Ginny sat in the chair covered in pink flamingos with her brown hair up in a high ponytail that seemed to start on the top of her head, and she said that when she got home she'd pray for me to stop drinking.

I didn't think I'd heard her correctly. But my heartbeat ticked up. The girls were asleep in their beds, and Lukas was at the hotel gym riding the stationary bike. Some time passed in which neither of us said anything, and her words sat in the room while CNN International showed live footage of a typhoon in the Philippines that had blocked out power in the country.

I loved my sister, and sometimes she could read my mind, but she could not talk about my drinking. "Don't pray for me, Ginny," I said. This was one of only two hard moments we had in Hong Kong. I didn't want her prayers, or her religion with no birthdays.

"Why don't you vote?" I asked her and tried to give it right back to her. It really did bother me that her religion didn't believe in voting, and I wanted to change the subject badly. She flipped through People magazine with the photo of Prince Harry on the cover, and the pages made a slapping sound. We had a stack of these magazines in the room, and I'd read them all.

Later, when she got home to California, she sent me an email saying she was going to AA meetings for me. I knew people told themselves stories to feel better, and maybe her story needed to be that she was going to AA meetings for me, but I didn't write her back for several months.

30

I want to say something about the drinking. For a long time I had a belief about drinking that was faulty. I believed you were either someone who could drink or someone who could not drink, and I thought I was the former. I didn't understand there were gradations, and that I was someone who seemed like she could drink but shouldn't have been drinking.

When we got home from Hong Kong, Lukas drove me to the secret shops where they sell illegal DVDs of whole seasons of Mad Men, and I lay on the couch in the living room and watched episodes for hours and hours. I don't know what this says about my longing for escape.

The man I pay to ask me questions in Beijing recently told me, "That was then and this is now. The past is not happening anymore."

I think he means I lived it, but it's over. My sister Margaret carried down the stairs. The hunting cabin in the woods behind our house. The man also said being closer to the pain can mean becoming free, and he uses words like this. "Free." They're embarrassing words that make me half-smile, and then I go home and hold them in my hand like stones I've found at the beach and want to keep.

I need to explain that I didn't come home from my Hong Kong surgery and just start drinking more. I'd already imagined that it was possible to drink more than I used to. What I'm trying to say is that I saw I might have a problem and then I made the problem worse. I know more about addiction now, but at the time it wasn't the sugars I wanted, or I didn't think I wanted them. I wanted the distance that alcohol gave me from my life.

When Margaret got really sick, we didn't talk about it the way you might think. Lukas says that it's almost as if my family is Christian Scientist, which is the kind of religion that doesn't believe in going to the doctor, and this doesn't sound so far from Jehovah's Witnesses, and in any case, it might be true. When my sister was sick, I wanted to be sick with her, too. I wanted the attention she got and to stay home from school like she did, but really I wanted to help her and to make her life my life.

I wasn't sad about Margaret in the way you might think. If what's happening before you—if your sister is getting very thin and also puffy in the face and doughy, and if she lies in bed and lies in bed and goes into a coma in her bed, it isn't really happening because you can't allow for that. You can't be sad. You can't be anything.

I see now why the man in Beijing was trying to get me to

distinguish between real and not real. Things I could control and things I couldn't. I once said to him, "I don't unpack those things. Please don't make me do that." In this way I was more like my husband than I thought, and I planned to leave this man I paid to ask me questions and never come back. The man said he could see I was a survivor and he wouldn't make me unpack all of my suitcases, but he'd like me to re-arrange things inside a few of them to get me better prepared for travel.

Sunday and Monday were more yoga and little sleep, and by lunch Tuesday I didn't want to be around any of the people in Shashan. This is the problem with retreats. There are always people. We'd done a different kind of yoga that morning called yin, where Justice made us hold the poses much longer, and it was difficult to do this and also seemed ridiculous because how could stretching be that hard?

Afterward, we climbed up the hill for lunch, and on the way Tasmin told me she had a famous French astronomer friend named Serge Honore who chaired the board of American Airlines and was willing to feature a photo of one of my paintings in their in-flight magazine. "All you have to do, Elsey, is come to my garden party and speak to him."

"I can't make it." Was she kidding?

"It's in two weeks, Elsey. You must meet him and convince him to take one of your paintings. It will be fantastic."

"But Lukas is away that week," I lied. "Some music event in Shanghai." I'd recently seen how I could paint the sky, but

I couldn't go back to my earlier work, and I couldn't meet with the man named Serge. I wasn't ready. I was in the process of becoming a different painter, though I didn't admit this to myself yet.

Tasmin made her tsk sound and sighed. "Elsey, I don't think you understand how busy these people are. How unusual it is that Serge is willing to do this for you."

"Oh, Tasmin, I'm grateful. Maybe in June when I know Lukas's schedule better."

She shook her head and wouldn't let me off. "I won't be here in June. I'm flying to Myanmar. You have to think about your career, Elsey. I've told you this before. And Serge. He's impossible to track down."

"I know it. I really do. It's just not the right time." Who would rescue me from her? And why was she talking about this in the mountains? We were on a retreat. Weren't we meant to be butterflies?

We got to the terrace, and Mrs. Liu cooked over the wok in the canteen and Mr. Liu went in and out delivering red peppers and chicken and rice.

"Let me just be clear." Tasmin spooned chicken onto her plate. "I don't believe for one second this country is communist anymore."

"It is true, Tasmin." Mei smiled. "We are fraudulent. We want Louis Vuitton handbags, and we want a strong proletariat, and we want to take over the world."

"I intend to make as much money as I can before the next revolution." Tasmin reached for the salad, and I stared at her and couldn't believe the words out of her mouth. They embarrassed me, and I felt sort of responsible for them just by knowing her.

"You should act quickly," Mei said, "before we kick all foreigners out."

"I'm moving as fast as I can." Tasmin laughed, but it was a forced laugh that pinched the muscles around her mouth. She tipped back in her plastic chair. "For God's sake, we are far from the city up here."

"It's why we come, Tasmin. To be far away. It's why I come, anyway." I don't know why I said this. It was affected of me, and I bet I was missing the city as much as she was and was trying to talk myself into not missing it. But she was grating, and I wasn't able to separate from her fully.

"You look like you're glowing, Tasmin," Ulla said and scrunched her eyebrows together, which deepened the quotation marks between her eyes.

"I'm eating a rare form of tree bark that's cleared up my skin and given me crazy amounts of energy."

I had to look away and bite the insides of my mouth to stop from laughing. Tree lay down on the ratty couch whose legs had been sawed off. Her forehead had a section of wrinkles through the middle that made her look older than she was. Two of the orange cats jumped into her lap, and she petted them and put her ankle up on the arm of the couch and closed her eyes.

This was the meal where I learned that Maeve was a sous-chef in a new French place near the Forbidden City and seemed to be sleeping with the Vietnamese woman sommelier there.

"Do you two drink wine together in bed?" Toby asked her and put several red peppers in his mouth at once.

He worked for the American clothing designer Marc Jacobs and wore many different-colored thin yarn bracelets on his wrist and a white shirt that looked torn in places on purpose.

"Do you always wear three-hundred-dollar shirts that make you look like an idiot?" Maeve smiled, and he kicked her gently under the table.

Mr. Liu placed a grilled eel on the lazy Susan. Black and charbroiled and horrible. I'd had nightmares about snakes that year, and now here was an eel, first cousin of snake. Thicker in the middle than at the head and tail. If my phone worked, I would have called Lukas and told him I hadn't had anything to drink, which was something, I suppose by day five, but that I was also ready to crack.

Justice spooned a three-inch section out of the middle of the eel and left the skin intact on the side the way you scoop out a Chinese eggplant.

"The biggest risk in a mine," Hunter told Andre, "is not from a flat, but from gas emitted from the explosion." Hunter had the slightly puffy face some people would think is handsome, and I could feel money around him. He reached for the eel and cut off a piece and seemed to not know what to do with it on his plate. I couldn't look away.

"A flat?" Andre asked him.

"An explosion. We do roof and pillar mining and you have to support your roof. No one talks about this in the Chinese press. It's the gas emitted from coal that explodes if it's not ventilated properly. Carbon monoxide is what kills the miners." He didn't smile often, and in some ways appeared to be the most out of place of all of us. I think he was like Andre and Tree and maybe Tasmin, who had all come for a vacation. The others were working through something in Shashan, or maybe all of us were and I couldn't see it. It was harder to tell than you'd think.

Hunter turned to Mei. "And you do what?" He shoveled rice into his mouth with his chopsticks, and some of the rice fell back onto the eel.

"I paint." Mei waved her hand in the air. "It is nothing, really."

"It is something," Justice said. "Her painting is very good."

Andre said he painted, too. "Landscapes of the Caribbean."

Mei nodded and smiled.

Andre said when he wasn't painting, he was head purser for Air France.

Mei didn't know this word, "purser." "You hold ladies' handbags on the airplanes?"

"You're joking, right?" Andre seemed hurt, but he recovered and asked if she was a model from Shanghai. "Because you are so thin."

Hunter asked Mei if she wanted more rice or some of the eel. "Once I learn more Mandarin," he added, "I'll understand real China. Until then you've got to put up with my English."

"Or you could take a Chinese language class." She reached for the platter of pork.

"You eat a lot for such a small person." Hunter smiled.

Mei shrugged. "Don't you know that we are always hungry in China?"

Hunter tried to debone the eel by poking around in the meat with his chopsticks. Then he turned to me and asked what I'd done in Dublin before I moved to China, and I couldn't remember. Maybe it was the eel. But I couldn't recall whole parts of my life. It was the first time he'd asked me a direct question, and I was surprised because there comes a point when you meet someone new, and if they haven't asked you a question about yourself, you know they aren't ever going to ask you a question. It's important to get this cleared up early with people, and I thought Hunter was a non-question-asker, so I'd ruled him out.

When he asked me about Dublin, everything about my life before China was blocked. I knew I lived with the man named Tommy and that I painted and left Tommy. But this all seemed vague and unconnected to who I really was. It might have been another part of the reason why I agreed to go to Shashan—the vagueness of my history and my willingness to bury the things I felt.

After yoga Tuesday night, Justice asked us to sit on the rug and press our back against the back of someone else and close our eyes until our breathing pattern matched our partner's breathing pattern. Hunter sat down with Mei, and I thought Tree would choose Justice because she always got to him first, but Andre asked Tree before she could ask anyone else. Tasmin was with Toby, and Ulla sat with Adrian. Maeve lay down on the rug and closed her eyes and said she was passing on this one, so I was left with Justice. He and I walked to the back corner of the house, farthest away from the door, and he pointed to the rug and smiled again, and we sat down and maneuvered our bodies until our backs were pressed against each other.

"Take deep breaths," he said to everyone in the room. "Watch the breaths and the feelings attached to the breaths come and go in and out of your bodies. Notice also the weight of your body on the ground. The weight of your arms and legs. You'll be more attentive. More alert."

I wasn't sure. But I'll try to describe what it felt like to breathe with Justice: very, very intimate. It was like lying down in a bed with a stranger. His back felt solid, but also gave a little, and I liked leaning into it. We were meant to close our eyes, and I tried to breathe when Justice breathed, but it was hard at first because he took so many fewer breaths than me. I had to slow down, and it was beyond sex but also extremely sexual, and I was never sure he was feeling these things, too. I think not. I think he sat with people often like this, and that he was just open in his body.

He never indicated he was aware of me during the breathing, except he corrected his breathing each time we got out of synch. When it was almost over, he told the room we should open our eyes and slowly come back. I didn't want to come back. Right before he stood up, he pressed my hands with his hands, and I felt the connection with him I'd been waiting for since I got there. I thought he understood me, and I was grateful.

Then he announced that the day of silence had begun. "You are to try to be quiet," he said, "until the end of yoga tomorrow evening. Many things will come up, and you should write them down."

He bowed his head and put his hands together in prayer in front of his chest. "I wish you well."

· 33 ·

The next morning we ate fermented vegetables and hard-boiled eggs without speaking. Then down to the yoga past the barking dogs and grandmothers feeding the pigs. At first the novelty of it was something. How were the others handling the silence? Could they bear it?

At lunch the kang sleepers wrote little notes to one another on pieces of paper from a notebook Maeve kept in her backpack, and they passed the notes and became hilarious while they ate the rice noodle soup, and I envied them.

Mei chain-smoked on the couch and seemed to have no interest in lunch or being part of the silent people. After I was done with my soup, she motioned me over and raised her eyes and looked out over the mountains with a smirk, and I started giggling and couldn't stop for a minute and was sort of out of control. Not because Mei had really done anything funny, but because of my anxiety over being inside my own head.

After lunch we walked about a mile across the middle of

the mountain and passed the terraced fields cordoned off with tidy stone walls. We came to an oblong lake, which was also a reservoir, and Justice said we should spread out along the shore and in the field and continue our silence. As if silence was a verb and we were in the act of doing something other than not speaking, which maybe we were. I'm not sure.

There were granite rocks and mosses and tall grasses, and I sat down on a large boulder. Justice stood to my right, maybe a foot from the lake. "Some of you," he said, "will get stuck in the silence today. Please imagine a time of great fear for yourself. Then a time of great safety. Go between these two: fear and safety, until you feel the difference and realize you can always be safe."

He also said we were meant to think of our ancestral powers. What did that mean?

"Change," he added, "is always possible. Everything you want is right inside you."

This last part was appealing, but then I really had no idea again what he was talking about. Some people fell asleep at the lake after that. I sat up for probably an hour looking at the water, but I wasn't good company with myself. I struggled and worried about my arm and if the pain would become a serious condition I could give a name to.

I finally lay down on the rock, and this came to me: a trip we'd taken a year earlier with the girls to a music festival in Yunnan Province that Lukas was playing in.

We stayed at a Buddhist hotel on the edge of Lijiang, and

the hotel had moss-covered Buddha sculptures and stone paths. Lukas was convinced spiritual belief in China had been supplanted by toaster ovens and luxury cars, but the hotel did feel like a spiritual place, and my memory of it is clearer than almost everything else that happened to us in China. On the second day the girls played a game with a boy named Marcus from Zambia—jumping into the pool and catching a tennis ball before it hit the water. Lukas was good at throwing the ball, and he did this while Marcus's mother, a very tall woman named Osana, swam. I sat in one of the canvas chaises next to the pool and read the last five pages of a novel by Colm Tóibín about a high-ranking Irish judge named Eamon who becomes a widower and says he doesn't believe in one thing anymore. Just ashes to ashes. Dust to dust. When I finished, I shut the book and closed my eyes and imagined how it would feel not to believe in anything. The feeling scared me and I opened my eyes and searched for the girls in the water.

Osana got out of the pool and put on a long batik robe and sat in the chair nearer to me. I asked where she was from.

"My husband got me to live in Wales for fifteen years, and I grew quite wet. Three years ago I got him to come back to Zambia."

I asked her how much longer she had in Yunnan.

"Not long. Next we will go to Christchurch, New Zealand. We belong to a spiritual organization that is having its annual meeting there." She had a lilting British accent and an overarticulated way of speaking that seemed almost like a collusion. That's how I will describe it. Like she thought I understood her, when I didn't.

I asked her the name of the spiritual organization. I don't know why, except I was curious and able to act as if I had some idea what she was talking about, when I had no idea. She was a glamorous woman. Maybe I was trying to impress her.

"Subud," she said.

Again I acted like I sort of knew what she was talking about and nodded. "Subud?"

"We will all meet in Christchurch on July Fourth and have come to Lijiang to be indulgent." Here is where she paused and looked me in the eyes. "Besides. You never know when this life as we know it is going to end."

Our conversation had taken a turn, but I wasn't sure where exactly. I smiled and got the girls out of the water and wrapped them in the blue-and-white striped towels and put them on a couch under one of the white canopies with Lukas. Then I went back to our room and pulled my laptop out of its quilted case and read that two or three times a week people in Subud talk directly to God. To receive him, the website said, Subud believers clear out the furniture in their houses and there is yelling and dancing and singing. I sat against the teak headboard with the wooden ceiling fan whirring above my head, and I couldn't understand the part about the moving of furniture and the couches and tables and chairs being picked up and taken away. It reminded me in some way of the Bible club my friends and I started before my sister got sick.

We met at the picnic table behind our house and my mother got Ritz crackers, and we all followed along in the Book of Genesis with a woman named Tonya York who was the evangelical minister's wife and told us the rapture would come soon and only people who hadn't sinned would be saved. "Have you sinned?" Tonya looked me in the eyes, and I was sure I'd sinned. I hadn't heard of the rapture. Why had no one told me? Because it seemed big and like something someone should have let me know about.

I found my mother in the kitchen after my friends left and said I wanted to be saved from the flood. My mother was a social worker who ran a high school out of our house for teen mothers getting GEDs after their babies had been born. I already knew she wasn't going to let me stay in the Bible club. She lit a cigarette by the electric range, took a long drag, and put it down in the clay ashtray I'd made her at YMCA camp. She didn't speak to me until my father got home. Then she waited for him to light his cigarette, and told me to go up to my room.

On my way upstairs I asked her to let me stay in the club. I said it really matters to me and all my friends are in it and I'm afraid of the rapture, and my mother said I was silly to believe in those things.

· 34 ·

I remember that I closed my computer in the hotel room and stood up from the bed, and the bottom of the computer had made the skin on my legs very hot. I was warm all over my body and unsettled about what I'd read. I put on my one-piece and went back to the pool where the boy named Marcus was teaching the girls a card game called Pounce that involved individual decks of cards for each player. I knew the game would be hard for Myla and easy for Elisabeth and that this was how their brains were wired, and I wanted to tell Myla not to play the game because it would end badly for her, but I was already trying not to be so controlling.

I dove into the water and swam to the shallow end, and my skin was a little tingly when I surfaced. I think a part of me wanted to join Subud, though I can't say for sure. I've had other times in my life when I wanted to belong to something, and I was in a way going through a time like that again in China. I sat on the stairs in the shallow end where the water came up to my waist and stared at Osana. Maybe it was a dangerous cult, but I didn't see how it could be, because Osana seemed gentle. My husband sat on one of the white couches with Elisabeth in his lap, and the towel I'd wrapped around her head had come loose, and her hair had dried into a weird sculpture on her head that I wanted to paint. I still wanted to paint then, though this was getting close to the time when I lost the painting.

Lukas wore his long surfer shorts and a rumpled linen shirt, and his beard had two days of stubble. I desired him but in a more distant way I was still getting used to since we'd married. That morning the girls had run ahead to the outdoor breakfast by the beach, and my husband turned to me on the dirt path and ran his finger down the middle of my back, and just his doing that made the hairs on my arms stand up.

He showed Elisabeth how to fan her cards properly and hold the cards closer to her chest so Myla and Marcus couldn't see them. He whispered advice in Elisabeth's ear, and Myla pouted, so he put Elisabeth down on the rattan mat and sat next to Myla on the couch and reordered her cards and scraped them against his beard back and forth. Myla reached for her cards, but Lukas wouldn't give them back. He was too involved in the game now, and this happened frequently that we lost Lukas like this. It was endearing to a point—his curiosity. But he was also competitive and wanted Myla to win the card game, or, more accurately, Lukas wanted to win the card game.

What did my husband long for? This was before I learned

not to live the way he lives, on adrenaline. But it was after the initial rush of marriage and children, and I was questioning Lukas though I couldn't see it yet. I wanted to take both of the girls in my arms and keep them from the need to belong.

35

On Thursday morning Justice stood on the terrace and said he had an announcement to make. "It's a surprise, really." He pulled his hair back into a ponytail and let it fall on his shoulders. "I've been waiting on word from my monk."

I was almost euphoric that morning. The end of the week seemed near, and I liked so much that Justice had a monk he'd been waiting on word from, and I liked being in Shashan now that we were able to talk again and the day of silence thank God was over. I thought I understood something about Justice and what he wanted from us and what he was able to give us, but now I think it was more about what I wanted to see.

"It takes a day to send message by foot and a day to hear back, and I've just heard we have permission to walk to my monk's temple on the mountaintop two villages over. We will leave in an hour."

No one at the table seemed openly opposed to walking to the temple. We seemed willing, as if we'd known all along when we signed up for the week in Shashan that we'd be asked to walk to Justice's monk's temple. It took us probably more like forty-five minutes to get ready instead of the full hour. Mei told me she was worried about the walk, and she did look very worried.

She said she didn't think she had the stamina to make it. "I don't have a water bottle." She frowned.

"I have two," I said. Both were full of water. "You don't need to worry. We aren't going far. It's going to be okay."

"I do not have an appropriate coat or jacket, if that is what you call it. My sweater will not keep me warm."

"You don't have to worry about staying warm. It's very hot this week."

"But we are going to the mountains." She had a question on her face. "Will it not be cold in the mountains? I have never done this hiking before. I have never been in the mountains."

I wanted to tell her we were already in the mountains. That Shashan was the mountains. But I understood what she meant. "It won't get any colder where we're going than it already is here. I promise."

She nodded her head and looked down at the ground, and we followed the goat paths up around the first full curve of the mountain until we reached the sloped fields where the Great Wall looked like it ran all the way to Mongolia. We had to walk in a line. Justice at the front. When we got to the pile of rocks where Tree had fallen the first night, Justice climbed up on the wall. It was probably about eleven o'clock in the morning, and the sky had turned soft white. The hot wind made me thirsty, and I handed Mei one of my water bottles, and she took a long drink and handed it back.

"It was good that you told them the other day that you don't have arm cancer. It's important to tell the truth."

I looked at her closely for maybe a minute or maybe it was only half a minute, but she didn't look away. I was trying to figure out what was real in her and what wasn't, but I could only detect real and that she understood the risk for me in the Talking Circle. It was important to me to have tried to tell the truth. It had something to do with not drinking.

36

"We will walk for two hours," Justice said when we were all assembled on the wall. Big blocks of stone had broken off the sides and lay in the middle of the walkway, and I tripped on one. It would have been hard to fall completely off the wall, but it could have been done. Lukas didn't know where I was now that I'd left Shashan. What if something happened to the girls? I'm not saying that he was going to definitively leave me if I kept drinking, but I decided to try and stop drinking that day on the Great Wall.

The land around us wasn't untouched, and there were postage-stamp villages smaller than Shashan and cornfields where old farmers worked with donkeys. Earlier that year I'd met a British man at an art opening whose goal was to walk the length of the wall, which is really many segments of wall, and write a book about it. This man took people on trips where they slept on the wall in tents, and I'd wanted to go on one of these trips for a long time but was afraid to leave my girls.

The air smelled of stone and dirt and cedar like the woods above the state beach in Maine with the picnic tables and charcoal grates, which was a place we passed on our way to the ocean, and I was sick for home suddenly and then for Margaret. I wanted her to be alive with me very badly, even just for the afternoon, and I hadn't felt that kind of real physical longing for her in years.

Ulla paused to scan for birds and held her arm up in the air for us to wait. I wasn't used to being around people for this long, and I worried I'd say things I'd regret—things people say when they're not allowing themselves to be in the situation they're in and are trying to will the situation away.

I thought of a trip Lukas and the girls and I took two weeks after my surgery when he'd become interested in a jasmine tea from Hangzhou. Before we got to the tea fields, we walked past apothecary shops in the center of town with picture windows and glass jars with dead snakes inside. Lukas pulled the girls and me into one of the shops to learn what tinctures the snakes were used for. I went along with it, but my heart was pounding, and I wanted to get far away from the herbalist who pulled a snake out with metal tongs so we could get a better look.

We walked in the tea fields for several hours after this and lost Lukas to the landowners and talk of soil acidity and irrigation, and there were many species of poisonous snakes in that region. I let the girls run on the paths where the older women knelt in straw hats picking tea leaves, but I didn't get over the snakes or the feeling that I was seeing China through Lukas's eyes. Living his life. I wasn't painting, so I was sort of floating away. To paint with the recklessness it required was impossible, and I had no inventory left to sell.

My dealer, Bree, was patient and the galleries were polite, but their interest had waned. That night, after Lukas and I got the girls asleep in the hotel, I went into our bathroom with paper and scotch and a small case of oil paints.

I sat on the toilet seat and tried to get at something about the tea fields and wanted to turn them into women in green, bell-shaped dresses. I took sips of scotch, and when Lukas woke up to go to the bathroom, it was a little bit like a circus. At the time he was just very, very angry, and I had a sick feeling but couldn't pinpoint why. Everything was chaotic in the room, and I was loud. Talking all the time. I said things about how I couldn't paint and that I was scared and wasn't a painter and wasn't a mother. Lukas asked me what on earth I was talking about. It seemed like what I said truly surprised him, but I'd been asking myself these questions since the girls were born, and he hadn't seen.

I was a good mother, he said. A tired one who'd had thyroid surgery and it had been a mistake to bring me to Hangzhou, and could I please be quiet or I'd wake the girls.

Then I did wake them. It was completely dark outside. Probably three a.m. I didn't know that I swore at Lukas in front of the girls or that I sat on the bamboo floor at the foot of their bed while they cried and said they would all leave me soon, and that I was nothing. Lukas has only recently told me these details. All I remembered was the shame in the morning. We gathered our things to go to the airport, and he said I was still recovering from the surgery. We didn't talk about the confusion I'd put them through in the night, but I'm sure he felt it and the girls did, too.

37

On the wall Mei told me she hadn't slept with any boys in her village, but when Leng hid in the room over the family's pig's stall she knew she'd sleep with him. "I was sixteen." She laughed.

"Ha. I knew nothing about sex. Imagine. I had the embarrassment after I did it. Yes. But I was also proud I had done it because I loved him. He had not been a student leader, but he had lived in the square for the seven weeks of occupation."

Her hair was up in one of Tasmin's white Nike baseball hats, and she walked slowly, so that everyone passed us until we were at the back of the line. She told me there were arguments about whether to leave the square or not and that Leng had gotten shot near the Avenue of Peace after he'd left. "His friends drove him three days and three nights. When the police came on the fourth day, they arrested my father for helping the boy, but they could not find the boy." She stopped to catch her breath.

"I do not know what this really means, hiking." She

laughed, and whenever she did this she seemed much more open. "Hiking?"

"How did the police find Leng? You can't skip that part."

"Oh, I forget each time that you are being interested. He worked in a coal mine in Yima County. Another miner turned him in to get the reward."

Leng went to prison for two years, and after he was released he wasn't supposed to travel in China for a year but he went looking for Mei. "For me. He came looking for me, and my future was being made now because he is a very forceful person. Very determined is what you would say in American. Our apartment in Guangzhou was small. Elsey, it was a small room. We worked in the computer-chip company. I was twenty-five and twenty-six and twenty-seven and twenty-eight."

"Computer chips? That's funny to think of. You there."

"Funny? It was not funny. It was our lives. It was a chance for us. This factory. We knew it. We worked very hard, Elsey."

I wanted to say I'd thought it was funny as in unusual, not funny ha-ha. And I told her I hadn't meant to be insulting, but she didn't turn to look at me or acknowledge what I said.

Her photography exhibit was called "New Chinese Women," and it received good international reviews and one in the New York Times that compared her to the American artist Cindy Sherman and said Mei was at the forefront of a reexamination of women's art in China. The photographs carry great emotional charge: Chinese woman as prostitute,

Chinese woman in collarless jacket for the Long March, Chinese woman in gray wool blazer. Mei was obsessive about details and color and light. In one photograph she wears a long, dark wig and a red qipao and lies on a velvet settee, head against the pillow. An older white man begins the act of unbuttoning her. You see the man only in profile. There are dozens of them. Maybe the woman's body as barometer of China's progress.

"I thought I would have babies but it never happened," she said. "I think it was what a religious person would call a blessing."

"I am sorry."

"Do not be sorry. You Americans are always sorry for something. It is what happened. I did not have the babies and later I did not want the babies because I had nothing to stop me then from my painting. You see? I had no excuses."

I stared at the back of her head. Stared and stared. Did she know I had excuses? How could she have not seen that?

We stopped at a watchtower, and the whole group got out water bottles and slugged. The land around that part of the wall looked like tinder, and Justice said twenty more minutes until the temple. We started walking again. Mei said after the computer chips, she'd worked at a factory that made underwear for a place in America no one had heard of called the Gap, and Leng cooked pork in their apartment on the electric burner. "Now Leng is famous, no?" She said this last part like a statement-question. "He has friends with officials but also with activists."

The year before, a large museum in New York had asked him to curate a Chinese retrospective, and he hadn't chosen any women artists. Not even Mei. "My husband does not like the female artists. He says he cannot detect any methodology in our work. Can you imagine that, Elsey? Can you imagine being married to this man?"

She stopped and turned and looked at me. "I will make a new life. Maybe I will kill him first for falling for the girl."

38

The sky looked like rippled skin on the ocean before a storm, and the group paused for more water. We caught up, and Tasmin asked Andre why only certain first-class Virgin Air cabins had fully reclining seats that turned into beds.

"It depends on the body of the aircraft," Andre said, and I cringed a little for him.

"Some first-class planes to London are a complete nightmare," Tasmin said when we began walking again. "You pay the same money, no matter whether you get the bed or not."

"Only the newer aircraft have that bed-seat configuration." Andre slowed his pace until maybe two body lengths separated him from Tasmin.

Justice paused between two watchtowers and pointed to the mountains up above. There was a series of Chinese characters painted on the rock that he read out loud: "Long Live Chairman Mao."

"Every spring the mayor of the village repaints the characters," he said.

"What does that even mean?" Hunter asked.

"It means you are standing in the seat of the local Communist Party," Justice said.

Toby and Adrian laughed, and Maeve got out a cigarette and lit it, which started a chain reaction of cigarettes. Tree took close-up photos of our faces, which she later sent me and were scary to look at because my face is vacant.

Ulla wandered off, and when we caught up she put her hand out again to block us, so we stood on the wall in silence while she tracked a black bird with her binoculars, then swore in Swedish and let us pass.

Mei asked me if Lukas was a good man, and I remembered the moment in the parking garage where I'd seen my marriage in the reflection in the car window and hadn't wanted to lose it. I told Mei yes, my husband was a good man.

When he was moved by music, Lukas opened his mouth wide and stuck his tongue partly out and looked like he was about to yell, but he never yelled. He also sometimes put his arm up in the air. That's my first memory of him: arm in the air.

"Mine," Mei said, "loved me and then he was not loving me."

"Marriage is long. It is a work in progress." I worried I sounded cliché, or that she thought I was advocating for her husband when really I was stating facts. Marriage is long. I didn't understand this when I married. Or how time speeds up after you have children.

"Leng will go to prison soon and I will, too, if I don't leave."

"Why prison if he's building a show for the military parade?"

"They will tire of him soon, and he will make too much money off his paintings and they will arrest him for tax fraud."

39

Sometimes when I was drinking and not being honest, there wasn't enough of myself to go around. I did not know how to ration myself for each of the girls. I didn't, for example, understand how to calm Myla down when I left the house at night. It got so I couldn't go to the supermarket during the day without her convulsing. It frustrated me, and I had a hard time with it. Elisabeth learned to be quiet when I went out, because Myla made so much noise about it. Elisabeth has learned a lot of things by watching.

My sister Margaret grew up watching. I've blocked out much of that time with her, so I can only hope I was kind when I was her sister. Our house was one hundred years old, and the plaster walls cracked from the inside. Margaret got scared of the sounds at night and used to call out, "What page are you on, Elsey?"

We were both big readers. It kept us from being scared. My room was across the hall from her room, and when she asked me what page, I yelled back, "Seventy-two."

Then I said, "Go to sleep now."

"See you tomorrow," she always said.

"See you tomorrow."

I don't know why we used those words. "See you tomorrow" seems professional. See you tomorrow. I hope it was enough. I hope my sister knew how much I was trying for both of us. I think she did, because she always went to sleep after that.

40

I never fell when I drank. I never banged into a wall. Lukas told me he came home early on the Friday in April because of a small kitchen fire at the nightclub he was playing at. He said I lay on my back like a starfish, and he couldn't wake me. I was still drunk when Myla crawled in with us in the morning and explained she'd worn her black T-shirt to sleep so the bad guys couldn't see her in the dark. Fireworks went off behind my eyeballs. Myla told me she had a superstition that at least half her body needed to be covered up by the blankets so the bad guys couldn't find her, and I said I knew that. I already knew that.

"But could we do that now?" she said. "Could you cover me up better? Because I'm not covered up enough and need more of the sheet."

Then Elisabeth climbed in and I scooched over so there was more room for her between Lukas and me. "Mama, I was missing you," she said. "I was missing you, Mama. I was calling for you."

She had a throaty way of talking I haven't mentioned, so most of the time she sounded like she was from an early cave tribe just learning to speak. She took my face with both hands and pulled it close and pressed her nose into my mine. I didn't dare look at Lukas. I could hardly open my eyes, and I was ashamed and embarrassed by what I'd become. But for several weeks I did not stop drinking. That is what I need to acknowledge. After I'd drunk enough to pass out, I'd wake up in the morning and have regret but not exactly for the drinking. My mind was very clouded. A curtain hung there.

On the morning that Ginny left our hotel in Hong Kong, she'd stood next to her bed in the corner of the room she shared with the girls and said, "You'll know." She was putting the girls' clothes in small piles.

"Know what?" I asked. Lukas had taken the girls down to the hotel pool for a last swim, and Ginny was still mad at me for the night before when I'd asked her for a second glass of wine and she'd pretended she hadn't heard me. So I'd asked Lukas and he'd said no, too, I couldn't have more wine because of the painkillers.

I'd really wanted the second glass, and I told both of them they had no right to deny me and that I never asked for things, so couldn't they do me this one favor? But they wouldn't.

"You'll know when to stop drinking," Ginny said and went into the closet to get one of the girls' roller bags. "It will be when you can't bear the thought of waking up and doing it all over again."

My phase of concentrated drinking hadn't really started yet, so I didn't understand what my sister was talking about, and after she left I lay down on her bed and closed my eyes.

41

Lukas and I were hardly separated the first month we came back from Hong Kong. He was careful about work and took nights off and cooked things involving soy and ginger and fish that were so good. Myla wasn't as worried about me leaving to go anywhere because I didn't really ever leave the apartment. She was calmer, and it was as if those other times when she'd thrown herself at me never occurred.

But I had the nightmares and wasn't sleeping. I saw the future as a series of steps in which the girls would be in the act of leaving me, and then who would I be in China? The pain started up in my arm, and I lay on the couch and watched the girls zip their backpacks for the school bus, and my arm zinged and my thoughts were too persistent and close.

When I began drinking the Belgian beer from the convenience store in the basement of Tower Three, it was as if I'd had an affair. That's how Lukas later said my drinking made him feel—like I'd slept with another man when he found me drunk, and that he had a hard time looking at me on the mornings after the girls got out of our bed and I got up and didn't know where to start.

"I thought you'd get better and we would have our life back," he said when we'd gotten home from the tea fields. The glass shower muffled his words, but I knew what he was saying.

"We'll have our life back," I said and partly believed this. "But it won't go like you thought it would go."

I had to tell him this. I also wanted to tell him that my drinking had very little to do with him, but I knew he wouldn't believe me. I wouldn't have believed me, either, if I'd said that.

42

I've had enormous faith in him. He collects things that the Communist Army used during the Long March, so we have the soldiers' enameled tin cups and teapots with stars and sickles. He says he believes in accountings like this. The things. He won't go back to Denmark, even though his mother is in a convalescent home attached to a church, and I think it's hard to leave her alone for so long, but he's unmoved by me on the topic.

Sometimes, rarely, I've seen this other side of him, though never fully with the girls. It's an impatience that comes maybe from leaving his country.

He receives many gifts at the clubs and festivals where he plays, and he tries to give them away. Brand-name watches and silk ties and electronic devices. Receiving these things is formal and ritualized in China, and when you receive a gift it's meant to indebt you to the person who gave you the gift forever. I've watched my husband closely, and I don't think Lukas is indebted to anyone, and I don't think he's been changed by the gifts he receives.

I see the entitlement around us and am not immune. When Myla was five and Elisabeth was four, we asked them to begin riding the bus to school. Or we didn't ask them as much as tell them, but for it to work they had to agree. It was a big white coach bus with the word SUPER stretched across the right side and three large steps covered in black rubber you had to climb to get inside. For months the girls were old enough to ride the bus but wouldn't ride the bus. Myla was too scared to do it and often asked me during those months if she should be stressed about riding the bus. She was five years old, and it pained me to hear her use this word, stressed, because what did she have to be stressed about?

I've learned from her teachers and from the man who I pay to ask me questions that many children have worries and that Myla and Elisabeth are no different. They're trying to understand their place in the world. Once Myla rode the bus, Elisabeth rode it, too, because she'll do anything if Myla does it. But during this time when no one rode the bus, I used to drive the car at noon to get Elisabeth at her preschool attached to the elementary school inside the metal gate. It was complicated to get her out at noon, because no one else got out then. Everyone else in school went full-day. Getting out at noon involved finding the principal, who had to sign a slip that we had to give to one of the uniformed guards. But first I had to find Elisabeth's teacher to get the slip. Mrs. Carter was from England and very fair, and she let Elisabeth make the paintings of pink flowers with Lena that we still have on our walls.

One day I couldn't find the principal or get the form signed, so Elisabeth and I couldn't leave the grounds and it became frustrating. When I finally found Mrs. Carter I said, "Why is it so hard to get the form signed for half-day release?"

She smiled at me and looked very tired. "But, Elsey, we do not have a half-day release here. All the children go full-day."

After that Elisabeth went to preschool the full day. I didn't have to be the person who created her own half-day program for her child. And it wasn't long until both my girls rode the bus. The bus driver spoke no English, but he waved at me whenever I waved at him, and I did this every morning to signal to him that my girls were getting on his bus and they were connected to someone. They were connected to me. I know if I hadn't become someone who sent her children to full-day preschool, I couldn't have kept my marriage. Don't ask me what the two things have in common, but there's something there.

43

After my sister died, my father retired from the bank and began building windmills in the field behind our house. Three of them. Life-sized and painted red. Then he had an affair with a thirty-year-old girls' basketball coach named Tammy Plover, who was also a teller at Augusta Savings. My mother learned of the affair after my uncle Whit, a man who spent most of his life teaching high school English in rural Vietnam, found my father behind Tammy's trailer on Carriage Road with a shotgun in his right hand. Uncle Whit told my mother that my father planned to shoot himself with this shotgun.

Uncle Whit died almost twenty years ago, and the funeral reception was held at Eady's Pub on the river in Hallowell, where people could dance to piped-in Irish music, though no one did this, thank God. The funeral was the start of the time when my parents began going to the Congregational Church and it helped. It seemed like they needed church, and maybe I'd needed it, too, which was why I was envious of Osana, the woman at the hotel in Lijiang who moved the furniture away to receive God.

My mother became active in her congregation, which was Tonya York's husband's church, the woman who'd started our Bible club years ago, but my mother seemed to have forgotten all of that. When I asked her about it at Uncle Whit's funeral, she said Tonya York sang in the church choir and had the most beautiful voice. "Like a songbird," my mother said and smiled, and that was all she had to say on the subject.

"Go get your father and take me home," she said some minutes later and reached out her hand so I could pull her from her metal chair. "I need to lie down with my Margaret."

I was twenty-two years old and about to move to Ireland. Nothing in my sister's room had been removed. My mother kept the same sheets on Margaret's bed, and it was a place she often went to lie down in. None of us questioned her about the room. None of us dared. My father drove us home from Eady's that day, and I saw maybe for the first time how clearly my mother held herself apart in her grief, and I didn't want to be like that. Separate.

· 44 ·

The part of the Great Wall we were on was mostly in ruins and it became impassable, so we had to get down and cross a pasture where black pigs stood in the mud. A wooden hut had been built into the side of the hill, and two barefoot children stood near the door and stared at us. It was a ten-minute walk to the temple from here, and the sky was dark like the inside of a steel bell. We stayed up on the ridge, and Mei said, "It will not be long before I am going to bed with the American."

I laughed and thought she was joking and was glad to be with her. I envied her life and wanted it. She made me feel it was possible to paint again, and though none of this makes sense now, for a short while I had no other life than my life in Shashan.

"I have never slept with any man except Leng," she said with her same matter-of-factness, and smiled and wasn't embarrassed.

Lukas once told me that he was playing music at a secret club for a senior Party official who appreciated Western music, and the official got very drunk so it was hard for him to sit up. The young girl who served the beer to him had an uneasy time, and there was, as there often is in China, the hint of sexual subservience. The older woman who ran the club told Lukas she needed to leave early because she was having an abortion. She and Lukas had known each other for almost ten years, and she spoke about the abortion casually, like she was going on holiday, and he was relieved by how clear she was.

The Great Wall was the color of iron on this part, and the kang sleepers hardly stopped talking while they walked and sounded like siblings. I missed my sister who wasn't alive and my sister who was alive, and realized you could miss people you hadn't seen in a long time just as much as you could miss people who were dead. I was far gone to my girls by then, but I knew they were okay because of the talk I'd had with Mei about telling the truth. Sometimes I vow to stop putting hope in other people like this, but then I meet someone like Mei.

We took a path through a field of apricot trees into a darker forest of cedar and pine and low-lying brush with dried-out branches. Ulla thought she saw the Mongolian hawk and put her arm out and made us stand still in the woods, and we couldn't speak while the bird sang its little song and Ulla stared through her binoculars. Then the bird flew away. "A very large warbler," she said and made a remark in Swedish that was probably like dammit.

We started walking again, and Hunter told Andre that his father co-owned a number of coal mines in China, all of which needed new carbon-monoxide monitoring systems, and which the father had sent Hunter to implement. He laughed then. Maybe because it seemed difficult to monitor many things in China.

When we got to the temple, it wasn't one temple but several stone buildings inside a grassy clearing. Some of the buildings were shaped like cones or rounded pyramids, which Justice said were tombs for dead monks. The larger building was made of paler stone, and Justice took us inside to look at a large wooden Buddha head that appeared recently painted. The top of the head almost touched the ceiling, and Justice stared at it and smiled with pride, and I smiled, too, but had the feeling I sometimes get in China that I'm meant to rise to the occasion and am falling short.

I walked as far away from the group as I could and found a fir tree behind the largest tomb. Justice called this an hour of silence and we weren't supposed to speak again. If a thought came into our minds, we were meant to acknowledge the thought and let it go. It was harder than I imagined, but I did sit for an hour and my thoughts had to do with the suspicion again that my left arm was being zapped.

Then I remembered a girl I'd seen once in Dublin standing next to the cemetery gate with reading glasses on and a purple cloth purse. She wasn't wearing any shoes in October, and we'd already had one light snow. She stepped into the street and put her hands out to steady herself the way you do on a trampoline. The cemetery was one block from the house where I rented my rooms, and it wasn't the kind of neighborhood with foot traffic because there wasn't any commerce. A short-term homeless shelter had opened next to a nearby chicken processing plant, and people at the shelter took the walking path up to the part of the cemetery near my rooms to do drugs, and I wondered if the girl had done that.

I stopped the old Renault, and the girl climbed into my backseat without seeing who I was. She wore nylon shorts with a flower design and a tank top, and I could have been anyone picking her up in my car. Movie trailers began to play in my mind of her being hurt by different men, and these trailers reminded me of the murders I used to imagine in our house at night in Maine.

"It's not safe out here," I said very clearly to her. "How did you get here?"

She said she wasn't sure, and her talking wasn't slurred, but she couldn't sit up straight or keep her head upright except by pressing it against the car window.

"I still don't understand why you're out here," I said and asked her again where her friends were.

Then she tried to get out of the car while it was moving, so I locked her in from the inside and she didn't protest and her passiveness made me feel ill. I knew I would have been like that, too, if I was as high as she was—I would have acted like everything was a little funny. But whether she was aware or not, things were still happening to her. We were still driving down behind the hospital. When I was drunk in the morning in Beijing, things were still happening. My girls still called for me from their beds down the hall, and their heart muscles pumped blood through their veins to keep them alive.

I stopped the car and unlocked it, and the girl got out and tried to take a wool blanket from my car and a novel about an arranged marriage in India in the 1920s. I put the car in park and climbed out and stood in the street next to her. "Give me my things," I said.

She looked confused.

"Why are you taking my things?" I felt a different kind of anger than when I'd seen the movie trailers of the men doing unspeakable things to her. I took my novel from her and the blanket and said like she was a child again, "These things are mine."

I was tiring of her, and I wonder if this is how Lukas felt when I didn't stop drinking after the first time he came home and saw me lying like a starfish in our bed.

She probably didn't live in the white apartment building across from the chicken processing plant where she said she did. Maybe she'd been left at the cemetery to sell her body. That seemed to be the reason, and it was easier to leave her after she'd tried to take my things. I said some warning words and tried to be strict and serious and ended with "Don't ever do this again."

She wasn't listening and didn't seem to hear me. I couldn't know how hard the people who loved her tried to help her, or if she even had people. I got back in my car and drove home, and I never saw her again.

A wet mist settled over the temple like smoke, and I couldn't see ten feet in front of me. Then the rain came, and the wind made the whooshing sound it makes when it's gathering. Justice found me at the fir tree and said he didn't like the wind and that we needed to leave. "Sand is coming," he said. How did he know that? He wanted us to walk down the mountain a mile to Yinfu, where Mr. Liu would have a van.

Mei stood under the pagoda with the ancient bell, and she looked very worried when I got there. Hunter also came and stood by the bell—many of us did, to get out of the rain. Hunter put his arm on Mei's shoulder, and this was when I saw that they were going to sleep together, and it interested me more than the storm.

Justice made us leave the pagoda and cross the field and get back up on the wall, which became slippery. After the first thunder, he pointed to a stone staircase on the side of the wall, and we all climbed down again. The path we were on was steep, and Mei struggled in a pair of Nikes that Tasmin loaned her that were too big.

"I am not liking the storm," she said, and I thought she might cry.

"We will be okay. Really, we will be okay."

"You just say that. You just say things to make people feel better. It is very American of you."

The thunder seemed like it was directly over our heads, and there was sand with the rain that landed in our eyes and mouth. I tried to walk carefully. I didn't want either of us to fall. It got colder and the day turned to dusk, and you couldn't hear to talk. Mei held on to my arm, and when the lightning hit maybe a hundred yards away, she started yelling in Mandarin and took off. I could see her small ponytail and then I couldn't.

Justice called out that she had to stay with the group. "It is safer!"

Hunter ran after her, and when I caught up thirty minutes later they were walking in the rain and holding hands and something had shifted between them.

· 46 ·

"Why." Andre stomped past me in the mud. "Are we even here? Why are we doing this?"

It was the first time I'd seen him angry, and it surprised me. What were we doing there? The weather pulled me out of my worry over my arm. I kept losing my footing. Most of us left the path at this point and walked on the rocks and brush along the side where it was drier. It was still too windy to really talk, and my heart pounded. We were on the mountain next to the mountain Shashan was on, and it had the same view of low-lying hills and the reservoir and clay rooftops, but we couldn't see any of that through the rain.

When Tasmin fell, it didn't look like a problem at first. She was one of the only people who hadn't gotten off the mud path. But once she fell, she began sliding. She screamed several times, and all Mei and I could do was stand to the side and watch. To really slide down the whole mountain would have meant a long way and many rocks, but there was nothing for her to hold on to. Her feet were out in front, and she was half on her side, half on her back, ponytail in the mud. She tried to stop herself on some of the larger rocks, but they were too big to hold on to.

Andre was near the front, and he threw himself at her and got her around the stomach. Then we all sidestepped down. The rain fell on her face, and she didn't move at first. Her poor arm was bent awkwardly, with her hand folded under her wrist.

Tree kneeled and wiped some of the mud off her cheek, and Tasmin said, "I'm the sickest I've been in years."

Ulla took her head in her lap and held it. "Silly woman. Why didn't you tell us you were sick?" It was the most affectionate I'd ever seen Ulla.

Then Tasmin turned over on her side and vomited. Her arm was still bent, and when Justice kneeled and tried to move her, she yelled, and Ulla said the men needed to carry her.

They took turns doing this, and I talked to her while they walked with her and told her that we were almost there. I said I'd find her some Sprite, because Sprite had always helped me when I was sick. "We're lucky," I said, "that Sprite seems like one of China's national beverages, and I'm determined to get you some." The rain kept coming, and Tasmin never opened her eyes.

47

We got to Yinfu, and I left Tasmin with Ulla and Tree on a bench next to the fiberglass exercise park. Bright red geraniums had been planted in the dirt along the road. I didn't see any stores. Justice pointed me toward a house with a thin, coyote-looking dog tied up outside, and I knocked on the door while the dog growled. An old woman in a blazer opened the door and stared, and I smiled in the rain while she decided whether to let me in. She had American and Chinese sodas on a low wooden bench, and Chinese cheese puffs and taffy with neon-pink cartoon drawings on the packaging that my girls loved. I bought the two bottles of Sprite and carried them back to Tasmin, whose tracksuit was soaked and looked like latex. She was alive, though, and I opened a Sprite and brought it to her mouth and told her to drink, and she obeyed.

She took two more sips, and I put the top back on the bottle and handed it to Ulla, who tried to give me orders about how to walk through the village looking for a car. "Go now, Elsey." She spoke tersely and with a nasal tone, maybe the affect of her Swedish accent. "Quickly, Elsey." She didn't try to hide her annoyance with me. "Move more quickly. You must go through the village."

Ulla must have been like this in her job sometimes. So impatient she couldn't mask it. But no villager in Yinfu was going to give me their car. Was she out of her mind? It was hard to get anyone to even talk to me, and there were few cars in the town to begin with.

Tasmin placed her wrist on her chest and kept it still, but she was moaning. I stood up from the bench and told Ulla first I'd go find Justice, who'd walked off to look for help. "Based on what Justice tells me, I'll begin to look for a car."

"I am going inside now," Mei said then. "You are being crazy if you think I am going to stay outside in this storm."

There was a pool hall two doors down from the exercise park, and she went in there to get out of the rain, and Hunter followed her. Then me. The hall was run by an old woman in a burlap dress who sat on a bench inside the door. It was dark and dry and warm in there, and I went back outside and got Ulla and Tree, and we laid Tasmin down on the bench next to the woman. The others followed, and it became crowded and was quite dark, until our eyes adjusted to the kerosene lamps. The ceiling and walls white stucco and the floor dark wood. A pool table took up most of the room.

"Chips?" I said to the woman in Mandarin. "Dried fried pork? Tofu? Almonds? Apricots?"

She took both of my hands in hers and raised them up and down in the air several times and smiled. Then she walked into a small closet behind the pool table and came out with plastic bags of Fritos. Justice grabbed pool cues off the wall and handed them to Hunter and Toby and Maeve. Tree clapped whenever Justice sank a ball, and her excitement seemed to be more about Justice than about the pool. When she ordered a round of Tsingtao, I hadn't expected it. I hadn't considered it.

The grandmother brought out eight bottles on a white plastic tray, and I could have drunk one of the beers in a swallow and nothing bad would have happened to me.

Tsingtao was one of the national brands I didn't really like, but I wanted to drink one of the beers. I wanted it almost as much as I'd wanted to be the person to get Lukas the glass of water in the dance club. One beer in a pool hall. Everyone else was casual with their beers and sipped them like the beer was good but not something they'd risk husbands and two small girls on.

I moved away from the one beer left on the tray, which was my beer, so I was standing closer to the door when two men came into the hall and called out to the grandmother, and she brought them clear alcohol in thick shot glasses. I'm not sure if the grandmother had just put it on, but stringy zithers played from a tape recorder, and Tree walked over to the two red-faced Chinese men and began to dance. She'd drunk her beer and also mine, and the two men smiled at her, but it was more like leering. One pulled her close so they were slow-dancing, but the man was making a mockery of it with his facial expressions.

Justice and the kang sleepers kept playing pool, and Hunter and Mei stood in the corner of the hall farthest away from the door. They weren't holding hands but were connected by how close their faces were and how their shoulders touched, and it looked sexual without being explicitly sexual.

Ulla said, "Elsey, I think you should come sit down now."

How Ulla knew this, I didn't know. But it has stayed with me that she understood the room and wanted to help me, because the man who was dancing with Tree grabbed the tray our beers had been on and then threw it against the wall where Mei and Hunter stood.

"Now why did you do that?" Tree opened her eyes. "We were having such a nice time."

48

Justice put down his pool cue and walked to the man who'd thrown the tray, and the man lunged at him but was so drunk he fell on the floor. The other drunk man went to Hunter in the corner and tried to wrestle him and pressed his body into Hunter and used Hunter to help keep his balance. The grandmother waved her arms and repeated something I couldn't understand. Ulla got Tasmin to stand and put her arm around Ulla's shoulder. We moved her to the doorway, which had strips of clear plastic hanging that brushed against my face, and this was when Mei's husband, Leng, opened the door from the street side, so we had to move back to allow him in.

The fighting stopped when he got there. He was wearing the camouflage you buy in the malls that looks like real Chinese Army material. Mei came to him by the pool table and spoke loudly in Mandarin about why she was leaving him.

"I am no longer afraid," she said at the end. "I was never afraid. I was just ignorant." And he didn't touch her during this time and listened to her for several minutes. Then he took a butterfly knife out of his back pocket and unfolded it and began to move it around her face.

I tried not to shift any part of my body. Leng called out to the two drunk men and made Mei translate. "The stupid American will leave with my two friends before I kill him. And he will drive away with them. And if"—Mei spoke louder now—"I hear that he has seen my wife again or speaks to her, my friends and I will kill him."

"No," she corrected herself. "I said that in English wrong. It is me who will be being killed. Not Hunter." She smiled. The knife was still close to her chin. "He is not," Mei added slowly, "going to stand by and watch a dirty American fuck his wife."

No one said anything after that for maybe a minute, and I didn't want to take my eyes off the knife, but I also wanted to look at Leng's face to see if he meant it, because how could he mean it, but he meant it.

"Hunter, my friend," Justice said. "I think it is time you walked out of the hall and did as Leng says."

"It is with pleasure," Hunter said, but he seemed much older and vulnerable then, not only because of Leng and the knife but also because of the humiliation of being the one asked to leave. You could tell he wanted to stay.

Leng kept the knife pointed at Mei's chin and did not look at Hunter, only at Mei.

I wanted very much to leave with Hunter. I took Tasmin's good arm, and Ulla and I walked her toward the door with the strips of plastic, and neither of us asked Leng for permission. We were behind him now. Maybe two feet from Mei, but closer to the door, and I could reach out and touch the plastic strips. Justice rammed his shoulder into Leng's back, and the knife fell on the floor and Andre lay down and curled himself around it.

49

Outside, the storm had passed, and the sun seemed brighter for how dark it was in the pool hall. Ulla and Tasmin and I stood in a small dirt area next to the hall a few feet from the road.

"Jesus." Tasmin closed her eyes and reached for my arm. "Will someone turn the lights down and get me home?"

Leng walked out. Justice behind him. No knife. The two didn't speak. Justice turned at the door and went to Tasmin and took her wrist and asked her to bend it first one way and then the other, and these movements were very hard for her. Mei came out next, and Tree and Andre and the kang sleepers. Mei's face gave nothing away. She stood near me, closest to the road, and when Leng lit a cigarette and began walking, she turned from him and told Justice it was time to get out of Yinfu.

"It's true," Ulla said. "We should leave now, Justice. I see no need to remain here any longer. We cannot wait for a car."

But then the mayor arrived, and several villagers I hadn't

seen in the food canteen across the street crossed over. This happened a lot in China—the expats like a spectator sport. The mayor said we couldn't stay, and he began making a clicking sound and shooing us, so we started walking back down the road past the exercise park. The air got thicker and more humid, and Mei didn't speak. No one spoke, really. I had never been in a fight, which is testament to some part of my privilege and to the unpopulated state I'm from, so what happened in the pool hall was something dreamlike to me while it was going on and also afterward.

Once we left the village entirely, trees were almost all we saw for an hour. The road moved in switchbacks wide enough for two cars, and sometimes it seemed like we were going north again in order to go south. I thought we might see Hunter in a car by the side of the road, but we didn't see any cars. I also waited for Leng to come for us, because it seemed he would, and that this was the dangerous place he and Mei went together. I believed it was what they did.

I wasn't sure Tasmin could make it back to Shashan if her wrist was broken, because the pain would pull her whole arm and shoulder down, and it would be hard for her to walk. I slowed so I was next to her on the side of the road, and I told her that her arm would be okay if we could just get her back to the Lius'. Tears leaked down the sides of her face, so I rubbed her back while we walked and wanted her to know I noticed her.

50

After some time, a white van passed and pulled over, and Mr. Liu got out and unlocked the back door. We put Tasmin up front with him, and the nine of us climbed into the back and sat on the floor. The insides were black with coal dust, and we leaned on one another and pressed our hands against the sides to stop from falling over. Mei didn't speak during the ride. Even Maeve and Toby and Adrian seemed solemn. We parked in the clearing below Shashan and got out, and when I put my hand on Tasmin's forehead, her fever felt worse, but it was already dark so we decided to get her up to the Lius' and take her to the hospital in the morning.

Very few stars were out that night and I don't remember a moon, but maybe there was one. To carry Tasmin up the mountain Justice tried having her climb on him piggyback, and this almost worked because she was able to hold on to his neck. They kept switching off—Justice and then Andre and Toby and Adrian. I waited for Leng to step out from behind one of the houses where the dogs were tied, but that didn't happen, and I waited for Hunter to be on the terrace when we got there, and this didn't happen either.

When we got Tasmin to the top, Justice took her into her room and no one knew whether we should try to call her husband. He was involved in the British embassy—maybe the deputy ambassador or attaché. But how to call him? The cell phones didn't work, and it was nine o'clock, perhaps not too late to use the landline in the house at the bottom of the mountain, but we decided to wait. We were going home the next morning anyway.

It felt like we were partly abandoning Tasmin in her room by letting her sleep, but also like we were doing the right thing. We sat at the table after that, and Mrs. Liu had roasted two more of her chickens, and there were pork dumplings and rice and greens and dried shitakes reconstituted with egg and chive.

"We should call the police," Ulla said and took a dumpling with her chopsticks. "This isn't right. The men have kidnapped him and we need to report it."

"We are working on it, my friend." Justice smiled. "Mr. Liu has talked to the police in Huairou and Beijing. They are looking for our American."

What was Mei's face doing? I didn't look up from my plate because I didn't want to draw more attention to her. Crickets and frogs came out, and I wasn't hungry for any of the food and walked to my room. And even though I knew I'd leave in the morning and go back to my children and husband, I could only imagine staying in Shashan. We were all connected. I know I allowed myself to think like this only because I was going home, but it was thrilling to imagine a new life in China, and I have to admit this.

On my way to bed, I put my head in Tasmin's room, and she looked dead so I stood over her and watched the rise and fall of her chest under the sheet, and she woke up and I gave her more Sprite from the plastic cup I'd put by the side of the bed. The room was dark and hot, and she took my hand and tried to say something about the Sprite and how grateful she was not to be alone and how she missed her boys. I told her it was okay and waited until she was asleep before I backed out the door and closed it behind me.

51

In the morning everything was greener from the rain, and I wanted to go home. Tasmin appeared at the table looking pale and weak, and spooned porridge into one of the white bowls and sat next to me in the sun. "There was a moment," she said, "on the mountain when I was sliding, and I didn't know if I would stop. I need to go now. Can I do that? I need to see my husband. I feel I've run a marathon."

"That's the fever," Justice said. "You need to rest. And yes. We will get you down the mountain very soon."

Ulla said her driver would take Tasmin home, and Ulla stood and got a brown wool blanket from her room and tucked it around Tasmin's waist so her legs were covered up. She told Tasmin her body needed more heat than usual because of the internal injury. She sounded like a stern doctor. Had she also trained in medicine? Then she walked off across the terrace with her binoculars, scanning for birds.

Where was Mei? She was often first on the terrace in the morning and never this late, and I wanted to say goodbye to her and drive home. Tasmin's wrist was purpled and swollen, and Justice figured out how to make a sling from two pillowcases he tied together, and he got the sling over Tasmin's shoulder and under her elbow. She leaned back in her chair and put her feet up in my lap and closed her eyes, and I sat very still so I didn't disrupt her.

Andre brought out two decks of Air France cards from his room, and he and Toby and Adrian and Maeve began playing bridge.

"Has he been badly hurt? This is what I most want to know." Maeve studied her hand. "I mean, the men were animals. They were going to inflict some pain."

"It's fucked up." Toby picked a card from the deck.

"It's abhorrent is what it is," Adrian said. "We've got to get out of here and go help the bloke. I mean, where the hell is he?"

Tree came out of her room and poured herself tea and stood next to Justice at the table. "Are you really in a band? Is that why your hair is so long?"

"My hair is long," Justice said, "because I am a member of the Yi tribe and I do not cut it."

"We are not talking about hair now, Tree." Ulla turned and scowled and walked toward us. "A man is missing, if you recall?"

"I haven't forgotten. I just wanted to bloody change the mood up here."

"What else can the mood be, Tree?" Ulla asked her. "The man has vanished."

"It's bad business," Toby said. "People can't just disappear."

Mei came up the path then and sat down next to me. "I have left Hunter at the motel," she said and tapped one of Toby's cigarettes out of the pack and lit it.

The bridge players stopped playing, and we all stared.

"You've left Hunter where?" I asked.

"At the Double Happiness Motel." She put the lit cigarette in the corner of her mouth and reached for the porridge.

"Our Hunter?" I said and could feel my irritation rising. She couldn't be serious.

"How did he get there?" Andre asked. "To the hotel? How did Hunter? Was he not hurt?"

"My husband's men were fools." Mei's delivery was flat. "Idiots. They left him in Huairou, and he rented a car and drove back and found me." She smiled at this thought, and I saw Andre roll his eyes and Maeve begin to smile an unkind smile at Mei.

"Where is he now, Mei-Mei?" Justice used his careful voice. "Where is Hunter?"

"He is still at the motel. He believes things are more decided between us than they are, and that we will spend the rest of our lives together."

"How did you get back here without a car, Mei?" Ulla asked. "You didn't just leave the man, did you? Has it occurred to you, Mei, that we have all been pacing up here? Has it occurred to you that the police are involved and that Hunter might still be in danger? Jesus, you amaze me!"

"Ulla," Justice said. Nothing more.

But you could tell the logistics didn't make sense to Ulla, and they needed to make sense before she could understand them. "You had no car," she went on. "You couldn't have walked."

"The motel owner drove me. It was not a problem." Mei shrugged and took another spoonful of porridge. How she got from the motel back to the Lius' didn't appear to be of interest to her. Then she asked if she could come home with me to my apartment. "It is what I have decided. To fly to America."

"Yes," I said without thinking. I was angry, but I was also trying to appease her. I thought maybe the end of her marriage was causing her some kind of disassociation because of the way she was being so forceful and nonchalant. I'd known her for six days on a mountain, and who was I to say who she really was?

"Yes," I said again. "That will be fine. But what we want to know, Mei, is how Hunter is? How did you find him in the hotel? Hurt?"

"Hunter is very well." She smiled. "He is also seeking revenge."

Justice stood and said he was driving to the motel to get Hunter out of the valley. "It is not a place he wants to remain, now that the minders know who he is."

"The minders?" I asked.

"What are minders?" Maeve put her cards down on the table and looked at Justice.

"The men who took Hunter are not men off the street," Justice said. "It is a time of increased surveillance."

"Leng's men." Mei laughed and looked at me. "I told you he had sold his soul."

52

Mr. and Mrs. Liu walked us down to the grassy area at the bottom of the mountain where the cars were parked, and Tasmin and Ulla climbed into the Buick minivan with Ulla's driver and instructions to go to the Beijing hospital for an X-ray. Tree and Andre and the kang sleepers climbed into the white minivan. Adrian drove. Mei wore the black wig that reminded me of Jackie Kennedy, and no one was really speaking to her anymore, so our goodbyes were short. She and I got in my old Santana and rattled down the dirt road.

I couldn't understand how she'd gone to the hotel room with Hunter without telling me and how she'd left him there, and I wanted her to get some sleep in the car and to recover. We passed bales of hay and rows of corn and piles and piles of gray brick. After we made it out of the mountains, we saw small groupings of houses and more makeshift hair salons and automotive shops. No birdlife. The hawthorn and chestnut trees looked more orderly the closer we got to the capital, and I missed Lukas somewhere underneath my fifth rib.

I remembered how in Hong Kong my surgeon had been

running late for the surgery, and a nurse came by periodically to tell me the other surgeries my surgeon was conducting were experiencing complications. I didn't want to know what complications meant. Because my surgeon was late, I told Lukas to go to the lobby with the Starbucks food cart and make his calls about a music festival in Bali. I could still hit myself for letting him go. Lukas said he wanted to stay with me and hold my hand, but I insisted he leave. It was just one little node they were taking off my thyroid.

When I woke up, I was confused why he wasn't in the room with me, and I called for the nurse. In between sobs I told her that it would be great if she could go find my husband. "Lukas. The bearded man in jeans." I also said I seemed to be having some kind of anxiety attack.

The nurse was wonderful and from Australia, I think. "This happens more than you know, bub," she said. "We'll get through it together."

Lukas ran in and took my hand and told me he loved me. He never really left me after that except when I made him go check on the girls with Ginny at the hotel. In this way we were very close in the hospital, and we could have never separated again, but I was not able to maintain that closeness. I wasn't used to that kind of honesty.

53

On the way to the capital, I got the delusional idea that when I got home I'd have a conversation with the girls that would establish my love for them once and for all. I hadn't stopped to call Lukas to tell him I was bringing a new friend home, because I hadn't thought of it. Or what I really mean is I'd thought of it, but the idea seemed too complicated so I buried it. But even that might not be true. I wanted to surprise Lukas and for him to see I was better and that I had a famous Chinese friend, so in this way Mei was like a reward: Look what I did in Shashan.

She stared out the car window and said that during the Jasmine Uprising, Leng thought they might ignite something that would spread the way the Arab Spring had spread. "You know this phenomenon?"

"The Arab Spring, yes. But I'm confused about your husband's motives."

"Ha. He had a candlelight protest in Chaoyang and was detained for the subversion of the power. I did not know when he was going to be getting out. While he was in jail they made a new law that said it was forbidden to protest. They let him go after maybe six months but he was not allowed to discuss the beatings or what happened to his mind."

She reclined her seat and closed her eyes and after several minutes she started to make a fluty sound in her sleep. I looked in my rearview and half-expected Leng to be following us. No one was following us. I drove from the Fifth Ring to the Fourth Ring and got to Chaoyang Park, where you can see the top of the old roller coaster. Almost every city park in Beijing has an amusement park and this confuses me—the rides and pink stuffed bears for sale—because the city itself doesn't seem to have a sense of humor.

My cell phone worked. We'd been out of the mountains two hours and I could have called and Lukas would have known the name, and it would have prepared him for when she walked in our door. I should have called. I turned left and left again down the dirt road between the hutong and our apartment building, and down into the garage underneath. I was caught up in what had happened at the pool hall, and it all seemed important. To finally be involved in something happening in China. Because so much of our time felt peripheral—watching the government change hands again, and journalists leave. I waved to the man in the booth by the exit ramp and turned to Mei after I parked the car and almost didn't recognize her again in the wig.

54

Our apartment was the only stop on the twelfth floor, and our Chinese landlords didn't allow shoes in the hall, but they approved a wooden shoe cupboard. I slid off my sneakers, and Mei took off the wedge sandals, and we put them in the cupboard. Lukas was playing guitar in front of the wall of windows in the living room, and he didn't have time to put the guitar down before I got to him and kissed his face and had a jolt of longing.

"God, I've missed you," I said, and he laughed, barefoot and thinner in his jeans.

"You have a home, Elsey," Mei said. "It is a very nice home."

I'd forgotten she was there for that moment, and she walked down the hall into the living room and put her hand out to my husband.

"We have a guest," I said. "My friend. Mei Leng."

My husband didn't miss anything. "Mei Leng? The painter Mei Leng?"

I nodded, and Mei smiled and waved her hand. "No, no. I am not a painter here, I am your guest."

Lukas turned and they shook hands, and it seemed formal and funny to me that they were meeting. "I am a serious admirer of your work," he said, "and I forgot my manners. Can I offer you tea?"

"No, thank you. I am okay without tea."

"Where are the girls? Where are they?" I asked. The girls should have run down the hall by then, and my heart felt too big, and my longing to see them had become almost nostalgic, almost like they were people I'd known in my past and didn't really know anymore.

"Sunny has them at swimming lessons." Lukas rubbed his hand over his head and looked very tired, and I wanted to kiss him but I also was afraid of what he might ask me to say about my time away. "You didn't tell us when you were getting back, Els."

I sat on the gray couch that formed an angle across from the wall of windows. It wasn't going like I'd planned, and I hadn't been able to press my face into Myla and Elisabeth's faces. I couldn't sit any longer.

I stood and walked into Myla's bedroom and changed the sheets on her bed and moved some of her clothes into Elisabeth's room and took Mei into Myla's room and told her to rest if she wanted to rest. I was tired, and I knew I was obligated to her now and to this vague, outstanding debt I owed my husband.

55

I found him in the kitchen searing pork in the wok and humming a Velvet Underground song. "Els, you could have warned me."

"My cell phone didn't work."

"You brought her to our apartment and didn't let me know? I don't have enough food, and I have no idea how you are and it's all very sudden." When he spoke like this in fast declaratives his Danish accent was more pronounced, and it sounded like he was reciting a small list of my failures.

"She's not demanding. She doesn't care what we eat. We'll have the pork."

"Pork and what?" Lukas took a big sip of tea from his stained mug.

"Pork and rice. She's my friend. She understands."

But he couldn't get over it—that I'd brought her without telling him. He didn't ask whether or not I'd had anything to drink in Shashan, and the question sat between us and was everything but we couldn't touch it. We argued about whether to eat old string beans in the fridge, and I said yes, and Lukas thought no, they were too sad-looking. It was embarrassing, he said, to serve food like that to such an artist, and he won.

The man who I pay in Beijing says that in one sense, everyone always knows everything, and when I let myself believe this, it feels accurate. If everyone always knows everything, then in this way Lukas knew I hadn't had anything to drink but that I was thinking of drinking, and if I did drink, I planned to consider it a reward for the week in the mountains. I still thought like this then—in prizes.

Lukas kept humming his song, and I don't think I've mentioned the sound system in our bedroom yet, either. It's in the corner and is impressive and quite beautiful to look at in the way that looking at the engine of a racecar might be impressive if you are into racecars. He has two sets of headphones, and two leather chairs that face the turntable, and hundreds and hundreds of albums on shelves lining the wall. The night that Lukas had given me the brochure for Shashan he'd asked me to listen to a new song with him, and I'd put the headphones on because when he asks you to listen, it's an invitation to talk without talking. But I was tired and already so worried about having to go to the village that I took the headphones off before the song was over and got up and drifted away. I was sure the children needed something even though I'd said good night to them, and I wasn't as able as he was to sit in the chair and shut my eyes.

"You didn't stay to hear the end of the song," he told me when we'd gotten into bed that night and were deciding whether to make love, and I knew I'd already ruined something. He had his arms around me. "I made the song for you," he said. "I wanted you to stay and hear it."

The front door slammed and my girls ran down the hall, their hair slick from the pool and furred like seals. They buried their faces in my stomach, and I held the backs of their heads, and when they looked up at me they were okay and didn't blame me for anything. But neither of them had time to talk, because they were in the middle of the dog game again and began crawling on the floor.

Mei came out of Myla's room while the girls were still down there. "This is Mei," I said to them on the floor in the hall. "A painter who is going to live in America."

It had never been an idea of mine to have Mei in the apartment with the girls, but here it was. I made the girls pasta with butter and Parmesan, and while they ate, Mei asked them their favorite colors, and they thought on this and listed five, including their most most favorite, silver glitterfish. Myla's hair was springier while it dried, and her face was rounder and paler like mine. She laughed when Mei asked her what glitterfish really looked like, because how could you not know what glitterfish looked like, and she leaned her head into Mei's shoulder.

I watched each noodle go into their little mouths. Each sip of water. Their stories in between bites were long and involved: what happened at recess with a girl named Shua and an older girl named Lin, and the bad choices these girls made on the jungle gym. I worried that Mei found it tedious.

"Let's move it along, my pets," I said. "Finish so I can put you in the bath." It was only six-thirty.

"Elsey, why are you rushing them?" Mei asked. "They are not even being done yet. Let them eat."

She began singing a Chinese folksong to them about a boy with a long name called Tikki Tikki Tembo-no Sa Rembo-chari Bari Ruchi-pip Peri Pembo, who falls into a well and needs his brother to go find help to get him out. Sunny had taught the girls this song years ago, and they sang it with Mei and I hadn't known Mei could sing. Lukas came in from the bedroom to listen, and when they were done with the song all of us clapped. Elisabeth threw some pasta in the air and tried to catch it in her mouth and missed. I asked her to pick up the pasta off the floor and she pouted, but then she did it. Mei got up and refilled their water glasses in the kitchen and told them she wanted to watch them ride their bikes the next day on the paths around the apartment complex, and I hadn't expected her to understand them like this.

At bedtime I told the girls I loved them more than I could say, and Elisabeth closed her eyes and said, "I love you more than rocket ships." Until then they hadn't fully let me in. All afternoon they'd been relaxing back into me and the idea of having a mother, because it's a big thing, the idea of a mother. We hadn't had any delusional conversation in which I established my love for them.

"Sing me a rocket-ship song," Myla said, and I smiled. "No. No. Sing me a spaceship song instead. Please lie down on the bed. And take your hair down. No ponytails allowed. Take your hair down and sing."

The pain in my arm was better, and I didn't tell Lukas about it. How I felt about the pain confuses me now, but I think it was evidence that things could still get bad again. Lukas and Mei and I ate the pork with the delicious, almost burnt-tasting hoisin sauce he'd made, and they talked about how it was impossible to make art in the country now.

"I want to leave China and go to your America." She smiled at me. "Even though you are very casual with your America, Elsey, and someday your president Trump might break it."

Lukas tried to explain that once she left she'd be an exile and could probably never come back, or at least not for a long time. He sounded pedantic and condescending, which was unlike him, but she listened and nodded.

"You may lose your influence," he added, and I got irritated. Angry that he didn't know my arm hurt and that we didn't have any Belgian beer or bad sauvignon blanc in the back cupboards where I used to hide it.

"I have nothing to lose." Mei waved her arm in the air.

"The young people here care only for video games and Internet and cell phones. But the artists? The painters and filmmakers?" She lit a cigarette and put the burnt match on the table. "We can't make real art."

I saw again how she didn't have guilt, and I decided I wasn't going to have guilt anymore, either. I made a promise to myself while she talked that I would paint every day because she never missed even if it meant doing something small in a book she kept in her leather bag for this purpose. I also promised myself I'd hire Sunny full-time and have her stay until seven every night, and that I would go to my studio religiously and only join the girls later for dinner.

"Yes, Party propaganda everywhere." Lukas nodded. "It is not possible to question public policies."

Mei dragged on her cigarette and looked out the windows at the city. I was tired and wanted to write down the promises I'd made to myself before I forgot them. I thought they were important, and when we said good night I went to the desk in the back corner of the bedroom and scribbled the promises on the inside cover of a book on Mandarin verbs, and they'd already lost some force and looked overly complicated. Lukas came in and we climbed into bed, and at first he appeared so far away I couldn't see him.

I trusted the silence or pretended to trust it. Then I said, "I missed you." Because it was true.

"Oh, really." He began kissing my neck.

"Do you hate me a little for going away?"

"That's a stupid thing to say." He tucked the hair behind

my ear. "I want to hear now how it was. I want you to tell me everything. The yoga. The silence. Everything." When he kissed me, he tasted slightly metallic. He kissed me again, and I moved away and didn't speak, and he finally turned on the light. "So where are you now?"

"Under the fir tree in the temple courtyard, and I'm not allowed to talk."

"Come back. Our apartment is safe." He laughed. "You can talk here."

Then he reached his arm around my waist and pulled me to him, and I moved away. "Els," he said. "This is the part where you tell me about the mountains and the people. I've been waiting."

But I was tired and couldn't translate it. It was too early, and Mei was in Myla's room, and when this happens and I have too many people to please, I stop pleasing my husband first. He's the one who gets sacrificed.

"Tell me about the girls," I said by way of not answering him. "All about them."

"The girls are good. The girls are fine." He was saying that the girls didn't need me and were perfectly capable without me.

I wasn't more willing to look at things in our marriage yet. It's one of the worst parts to go over. I wasn't telling the truth about the pain in my arm, either, so no one in the apartment except me understood this fear. And it wasn't my arm that really scared me. I was afraid of not being there for my children, which may be another way of saying I was afraid I wouldn't be able to control their lives anymore.

"I'm not sure I can do it."

"Do what?"

"Stop drinking. I'm really not sure I can."

"But I thought you had. I thought you hadn't done any drinking since you got there. This is good. This is a start."

Maddening. Did he really believe it was as easy as that? "You didn't ask."

I cried then because of my certainty that I'd drink. It was easier to drink than to do the work required to not drink. I didn't know what that work was, but I could tell it would be hard and contingent on me. No one else was going to save me. It was silent in the bed after that for maybe five minutes and I almost fell asleep, but I felt terrible and far away and then I guess I did fall asleep.

57

Mei stayed at our apartment for a week, and I made many calls to the States for her and went wherever she went—to her friends' shops and galleries so she could say goodbye. On Monday we drove to Dashanzi to see her art dealer, a woman named Wu Lei who wore layers of red canvas clothing and had shaved her hair. She'd been to the States several times and was skilled at attracting Western customers for Mei's work, and she took us to the back of the gallery into a storage room with a cement floor, where a younger man in a dark suit coat poured us tea. Then Wu Lei got out her cigarettes and eased into her plastic chair and began smoking. She never looked at me, and I'm not sure she understood why I was there—the American. She was interested only in Mei and why she was leaving.

A lot of the time it sounded like the women were shouting at each other, and there was great emotion underneath the yelling. Wu Lei said it was sudden and would appear weak for Mei to leave, and could they not have one more show in which Wu Lei brought out all of Mei's work? A retrospective, she said. She needed time to bring it together. One month.

Mei said no. A month was too long. "I have lived with Leng since I was eighteen and I am forty now. It is not sudden to leave. I will be being gone by Friday."

Leng gave a talk on ancient calligraphy at the Beijing Museum. I think it was on Tuesday of that week. I know this because Tasmin went and called me afterward and told me Leng didn't name Mei exactly but he said Chinese artists who leave China are traitors who should never be allowed back.

"What are you going to do with her?" Tasmin asked me on the phone that night after Leng's talk.

"What do you mean do with her?"

"And Hunter. He's gone. I heard at the embassy party last week that he's flown back to the States. Was in way over his head."

"Hunter is gone?" I was repeating each thing she said and trying to store it in my head.

"Mei can't live with you forever, Elsey. You and Lukas will be questioned."

"Tasmin, please."

"No, really. She can't stay with you. You know that. She's too high-profile. She's too watched."

"Thank you for this." I couldn't hide my irritation with her, and it was the first time I was clear and let her see my emotion. "What am I meant to do, Tasmin? No, really. Please tell me if you have a solution, because I have none."

58

Several other painters and artists came to our apartment to say goodbye and to tell Mei it was good she was leaving Leng. They smoked in our living room, and I made them tea.

On Wednesday night, Lukas found me in our bedroom after the girls had gone to sleep and told me Shashan hadn't changed things for us.

"That isn't true. I'm different now."

"I wouldn't know if you're different because you're never here."

"I'm trying."

"Try harder."

"I haven't had a drink for fourteen days." I was proud of this, and it's hard to believe now that I thought fourteen days of not drinking was my crowning moment.

"I'm not sure it matters." It was at a time, he went on, when he needed things from me and to see if I was the person he thought I was.

I nodded, but I wasn't taking him seriously. It was as if I

had amnesia about how much he mattered. Mei had gone into Myla's bedroom to get a sweater, and she and I were going to the Baochao Hutong to hear Justice's band play.

"Where is Leng in all this?" Lukas asked. "I mean, come on. The man is too famous to let this happen on his watch. Couldn't he come and take her home?"

He sat down in one of his leather chairs facing the turntable. "I don't understand why it's you doing all of this for her. I mean, my God, Elsey. The man has to be wealthier than Mao. Isn't he going to come fight for his wife?"

I couldn't tell him about Leng and the pool hall and the knife. He would have been so angry and there was too much to explain. "We don't want Leng here. He's too complicated."

"We're all complicated. Tell him to come see his wife. Tell him she needs him."

59

The doorbell rang Thursday morning while Mei and the girls were in the kitchen cutting pictures of animals from National Geographic magazines. I was hanging wet clothes on a wooden rack next to the fridge because our dryer didn't work. Lukas had been set on getting our dryer fixed for months, and the landlord said he'd send someone but never did, so we gave up. The bell rang again, and I looked through the spy hole and saw a man in a black suit with a metal toolbox. He rang again, and Lukas flung the door open and began yelling in Mandarin that we'd heard the bell the first time and why couldn't he wait. "It is the polite thing to do! To wait!"

"I am here to fix the dryer," the man said in English. He was small and thick like a hydrant with a shaved head.

"We've been waiting months," Lukas said in Mandarin again, "for someone to notify us about scheduling the repair."

"It is a very busy time of year to fix dryers."

Lukas laughed and turned to me. "We have long given up on the dryer."

I hadn't seen my husband unnerved like this before, and I could tell he was tired and near some kind of breaking point.

"I would like to come in," the man continued. "I will not take long. I am very fast. I have tools." He pointed to his toolbox, and I thought Lukas might hit him, and I became worried that this man didn't know how to fix a dryer and had been sent to us maybe by Leng or who knows who sent him.

Lukas swore at the man in Danish and slammed the door in his face. And what got him, Lukas told me later in the kitchen after we'd walked the girls to the school bus, was that the repairman wouldn't speak Mandarin even though Lukas had spoken only Mandarin to him. "I've been in this country fifteen years." He looked out the one window in the kitchen. I saw how he'd made the mistake of thinking he belonged, and this was the rule, to never think you belonged here or were important, but it wasn't the time to remind him of this because I was still too far away for him to listen to me.

60

Mei packed her suitcase after Lukas left for the club, and the girls fought over who was taller. Then Myla lay down on Elisabeth on the rug in Elisabeth's room and kept her knee on her neck until I came in and found Elisabeth sobbing. They fought over who got to sleep in the top bunk, and when I turned out the lights, Elisabeth kicked the slats so hard she hurt her foot and sobbed again. But I was sort of suspended above my family. My life felt static next to Mei's. She was moving to Hong Kong, and maybe I wanted her life to be my life.

How the girls acted after I'd gotten home had been different than I imagined, and Elisabeth no longer let me kiss her on the cheek during the day, only at night before bed. Myla didn't seem to care if I came or went. I'd gotten a note home from her teacher that afternoon saying she'd spilled yogurt on her shirt during art and had changed out of the shirt and had worn just her zipper sweatshirt. But then she'd spilled yogurt on the sweatshirt, too, so she and the teacher went to the lost-and-found bin and got her another T-shirt.

"As you can imagine," the teacher wrote, "she was very emotional about this, but we did the best we could, and eventually she stopped crying. Her clothes were not quite dry when it was time to pack up for the bus. Is Myla upset about anything at home? She doesn't quite seem herself."

Before we went to bed, Mei had a cigarette on the little balcony with the glass railing where I never went because it was so high up it made me dizzy. She told me we needed to appear to be together at the airport. "Like family. We need to seem to be being related so the authorities will let me go."

"Related how?"

"Through marriage."

And when I raised my eyebrows, she laughed.

"As in you are the gay widow of my dead sister?" It was the first time I've ever used my sister in a joke.

"Well, not that exactly."

"It's in your documents, yes? Your marriage to Leng?"

"Yes." She took a long drag.

"It's better not to lie."

"It is decided then. But where is your sister, Elsey? I did not realize."

"She died years ago." I didn't say anything else. I had no interest in explaining it. Mei was leaving and needed the plane ticket and to withdraw more money, and we needed to focus on these parts of her life.

61

I told only Sunny about Hong Kong. I did not tell Lukas because I didn't think he'd let me go. At the airport I kept waiting for Leng to find us in the new terminal that's like a football stadium with the domed ceiling. Mei smoked a Yuxi down to the filter while we walked to the gate, and her hands shook while she lit the next one.

"I am not a fool, Elsey," she said. "I know that the plane is built to take off into the sky, but I cannot trust how it stays up there."

It was so bright in the terminal, it was hard to keep our eyes open. Shiny, square metallic tiles everywhere. At the gate a middle-aged Air China representative with a small vertical scar on his forehead asked Mei how long she intended to be in Hong Kong. It wasn't a trick question.

He said he didn't see a return ticket, and by law he needed to know when she was coming back to China, and I had to look away. I thought everything was riding on her answer.

"One week. To see my daughter. Then I return." And the man let her through. I thought she'd made it.

The bookseller's shop sat on a lane of chicken stalls and massage parlors and noodle houses. The bookseller, Justice's father, was a thin, white-haired man named Hong who smiled when he saw Mei and put his thumb to his lips and shook his head over and over again because of how much she'd grown. He sold trade paperbacks and romances and antigovernment literature, and he had a bedroom on top of the shop where Mei could stay while she waited for the American visa.

There were stacks and stacks of paperbacks on the floor and on the wooden shelves that lined the front room. A fat orange cat sat in the street window. Mei sat in the torn arm-chair in the back corner and smoked and waved me off. No hugging. We never hugged.

"Thank you, Elsey." She looked out the window at the traffic in the one-way street. "For being my first American friend."

I laughed, because she was trying to sound sarcastic, and she often said American sarcasm was something I'd made her better at. Of all things to teach someone.

I thought she'd get to America. The visa could take months. Or never. But she had many friends of friends who could get her jobs in Boston, and she was resourceful. She'd figure it out.

62

It was around nine o'clock when I got back to the apartment, and Sunny met me in the front hall and told me the girls had eaten pork baozi for dinner. "Liang ge baozi." Two each.

And they'd waited up for me. Elisabeth was in the bath, and Myla was in Elisabeth's room drawing. Sunny seemed excited—she was going ice-skating in one of the old bomb shelters underneath the city, which explained her extra eye shadow.

I found Lukas in the living room, and he put the guitar down on the rug. "Why," he said, "didn't you tell me you were leaving our children to fly to Hong Kong?"

How had he known?

"Were you drunk, Elsey? Tell me you were drunk. It's the only way I can understand why you wouldn't tell me. It's a simple thing. Telling your husband when you leave the country."

"I wasn't drunk." But I'd thought about drinking many

times that week and didn't have the tools to stop, so drinking was really just a matter of time.

He said I needed to go to the Alcoholics Anonymous meetings. "They have them in Shunyi. I've been researching alcoholics."

"It's a cult," I said, though I'd never had an opinion about Alcoholics Anonymous meetings except that they were something I didn't plan to do, the way I didn't plan to travel in space.

I followed him to the front door.

"You should go to the meetings, Elsey."

"I haven't had a drink since I left for Shashan, so your request is confusing."

"I'm taking the last flight to Shanghai tonight." He had a concert there over the weekend. "I may stay for a while."

"Go," I said. It wasn't even a fight.

Then I told him about the pain in my arm. "I've been really worrying over it. It's more than I can manage. The idea that I might be sick again."

"Nerve pain," he said. "It's nerve pain from the surgery."

Then he left.

63

I woke up alone on Saturday morning and felt exhilarated. In the afternoon I drove the girls south to Qingdao, and Myla acted like a little parent in the car and said things Lukas would have said: "Are you tired, Mama? I wish I could drive for you."

Elisabeth counted road signs until it got dark and she couldn't see them anymore and said her brain was hurting looking for them and she wanted to stop counting them but couldn't. I told her to sink down in the seat in back and close her eyes.

Qingdao looks out on the Yellow Sea, and I was trying to make a statement that I could drive there with the girls while Lukas was in Shanghai. But the drive was longer than I'd been led to believe, and the highway was flat and crowded with trucks and I couldn't see the road well and didn't know the way.

After the third hour, Myla became sullen in the passenger seat and asked if I knew where I was going. Her face took on masculine qualities of Lukas's face, and she started sighing like Lukas sighs.

Elisabeth said she had to go to the bathroom, but I wouldn't stop the car, because to pull over at one of the truck stops seemed too risky. I asked Myla to take my cell phone and read the directions to me out loud again. She was almost nine and read them slowly, but they didn't make sense.

"Are you reading it right, Myla?"

"Don't be mean, Mama. Don't be mean. You're worrying me."

"I'm not being mean!" My voice rising. "I don't mean to worry you, but I don't see how we go two hundred fifty kilometers west when we know that Qingdao is south!" I shouted the last part, and Myla cried, and I thought we'd never make it to the hotel, and even if we managed to, we'd never get home to Beijing or see Lukas again. It was full catastrophe thinking I hadn't let myself do for years—since after my sister had died and my family was not something I recognized. The kind of thinking that leads only to worse and worse thinking. It's like an illness, this kind of thinking.

Elisabeth slunk down lower in her seat so she couldn't see the road and couldn't count anything. "Daddy drives."

This wasn't true. Lukas didn't always drive, and I got angry again. Then a truck came up on us quickly and seemed almost to swallow us, and I yelled, "You motherfucking asshole!"

"You swear more now, Mama," Elisabeth said. "You swear much more and you're not supposed to." It was true. She was right.

64

We got to the Swissotel at close to seven and slept until eight in the morning, and we should have slept longer, but we were up too early and loud in the bed together and sort of nervous with each other. The room was square-shaped and beige and smelled of recent cigarettes. One rectangular window looked out over the city, which had a great deal of building equipment. Cranes and large bulldozers and half-built skyscrapers. It was difficult to believe on Thursday I'd been in Hong Kong at the bookseller's. It was hot in Qingdao. So hot and the air was still and pale white and thicker than air should be. We went to a tired amusement park by the ocean that had a roller coaster called the Express, which was small by Beijing standards, but the girls approved of it. My arm throbbed. I wish I'd known that the Hong Kong surgeon had nicked a nerve during the operation, but I didn't believe it, no matter what Lukas had said.

On the drive home the next day I checked my phone at a tollbooth on the Sixth Ring Road, and Lukas had called for the fifth time. I let Myla call him back when we got to the apartment, and I could tell from what she said that he was worried about us, but I wouldn't talk to him.

I told Myla to explain we were going to visit Ginny. "Tell him that and tell him I have the credit cards."

I've read now about people who act rashly in the weeks after they stop drinking. In some ways they are the most rash they've been in their lives during this time, because they feel invincible for not drinking. Irreproachable. Nothing can touch them. This was true of me. I'd made the decision to stop drinking, and then my life exploded. Lukas called me from Shanghai and told me again I had no business taking the girls to America. On Tuesday of that week I took the girls out of school and flew to California.

65

Two strange things happened in California. The first was that Myla and Elisabeth and Ginny and I took a ferry to Alcatraz Island, where a park ranger with a long blond beard met us at the dock and led us up a gravel path to the prison, which blended with the natural stone on the island so the whole thing looked oddly Mediterranean. There were about twenty in our group, and the ranger handed us black plastic headsets, and we started the audiotapes and began walking into the cells with the toilet bowls and enamel sinks.

Each cell had a metal cot and smelled of old urine, though there hadn't been prisoners for decades. I followed Myla into the third cell and the audiotape described several famous prisoners who had been murderers and lived in this cell and were later released. One of the prisoners was a man named the Birdman who spoke on the audiotape of watching men kill other men at Alcatraz.

He said it was a place of great desperation. He had a reedy, southern accent, which made him sound like he was in the prison leading the tour, and I became hot and mildly claustrophobic. There were windows in the cells, and Myla was struggling, too, but I couldn't see this yet because all our faces looked impassive while we listened to the tapes. I followed her into the exercise yard at the back of the prison, and Ginny followed Elisabeth. We didn't discuss this, it just happened naturally. You could stay longer in certain places if you wanted to hit pause on your audiotape, or you could move ahead. Myla kept moving ahead.

We finished on the far-left side of the prison, opposite the concrete cafeteria with bars on the windows, and Myla and I took the headphones off and gave them to the park ranger. When we walked outside, the fog was thicker and it had gotten colder. Myla was wearing only leggings and a Warriors T-shirt Ginny had given her, and I worried she would be cold. "Where are they, Mama?"

"Where are who?"

"The prisoners?"

"Dead," I said.

"Not all of them. Some are free. The Birdman is free." She touched both her ears with her hands like she was trying to get to the story inside the headphones, and I could see she was about to cry and that it had been a terrible idea to come.

Ginny and Elisabeth found us in the gravel clearing by the white flagpole, and I felt carsick the way I get when Lukas drives us too fast across Beijing. We followed the ranger down to the dock and got on the first ferry, and the ranger cast off our bowline, and Myla said, "Where are we going?"

"To San Francisco," Ginny told her.

"We can't go there," Myla said. "Because the men who did terrible things live there."

"You're confused," I told her. "None of the men who did terrible things are in San Francisco. They were moved to another prison when this one closed."

She was working to hold in her tears, and I took her hand and we sat together on the top deck, and our faces and hair got wet with the fog. I thought the four of us might never be together in the unconscious way that a family is together, and I was so sad for that and for not understanding Lukas better.

66

The second strange thing that happened in California was that after we got off the ferry at Fisherman's Wharf, a tall man dressed in long black clothing jumped out from behind a bush on the sidewalk and began chasing us.

"Run for your life!" Myla yelled, and I began running as fast as I could to keep up with her. Ginny and Elisabeth were behind me, and the man seemed to gain on us and to laugh while he chased us.

"Run faster, Mama!" Myla yelled. And I tried to run faster, but I couldn't keep up, so I stopped and turned to the man chasing us and became so angry I couldn't form words at first. I swore at him and pointed and told him if he came any closer to my children I would hurt him. Tourists were buying Italian ice on the sidewalk, and how did they not see the man who meant to harm my children? The man stopped laughing, and I kept pointing and jabbing the air with my finger, and he turned and went back to his bush.

"Slow down," I said when I caught up to Myla, and my

arms were shaking and my legs. "It's okay now. It's okay, the man is gone."

There was a Five Guys a block away, and we went inside, and Elisabeth was worked up and cried at our table in the corner, but I don't think she was as scared as Myla was. I ordered everyone burgers and fries and got the brown paper bags of peanuts that come with the burgers, and Ginny said she'd heard of these men, and people in the city were mixed.

"Some people like them and the way they scare people. They give the men money."

"Money?" I said, and she nodded. Then we didn't say anything more about the man. We ate our burgers and drove home, and when we got back to Ginny's house south of the city, neither Ginny nor I could have a drink because we were no longer drinking.

67

She lived in a semidetached stucco subsidized by the Air Force, where her husband was a senior officer doing things involved with engines and airplanes. When Steve came home, we bowed our heads at dinner and prayed. I was worried one of the girls, maybe Elisabeth, would not be able to go through with the praying, but Steve was regular and clear on the praying, and we managed it.

We'd climbed the Twin Peaks that week and rented bikes on Crissy Field and ridden them to the trampoline park by the Golden Gate Bridge, and it had been a surprise to me how good it was to be with the girls and Ginny and her family, so there was relief in that for me. But it was also a time of pretending, because I was missing Lukas so much and not telling him this, and I knew he'd be angry with me for leaving.

Not long after dinner, the girls and I went down to my niece Charlotte's room in the basement and Myla said she needed to tell me about the prisoners who'd been released from Alcatraz. She said she didn't think San Francisco was a safe place and that we needed to leave and go back to Daddy.

"Where is Daddy?"

Around two in the morning, she began sobbing, and I held her in my arms. "Shhhh. You're going to wake up Elisabeth."

Myla cried and cried in my bed, and I still didn't fully give in to her. How do I say this? After Margaret died, I learned you never told how bad it was, and I think this was one reason I wasn't able to fully comfort Myla at first. She finally woke up Elisabeth down on her air mattress, and she climbed into our bed. Then both girls were crying, and I was too tired and didn't care anymore if we woke up Ginny and her husband in their paneled room off the kitchen upstairs. I didn't try to tell the girls they weren't sad or that they didn't miss Lukas because I knew they missed their father and that this was part of why Myla felt so unsafe.

I was scared for Myla, and I hugged them both and cried for how scared we'd all been on Fisherman's Wharf, and it was a start. I made a plan to call Lukas in the morning and tell him we were coming home and that Alcatraz was a mistake and leaving him was a mistake. But what if Lukas had a lover in Shanghai? I hadn't slept. I wasn't thinking clearly.

I knew I had to be patient and wait for him to return to me, and I'd gone to America to be patient. Charlotte's room had one poster of many white kittens in a straw basket, and I stared at that poster while light came through the metal grates on the window. All I could think of was how until I met Lukas I hadn't thought I should be a mother. I was afraid children would ask more of me than I could give. Margaret had asked more of us than we could give her. We hadn't been able to save her.

When I woke up again it was seven in the morning, and I wanted to call Lukas but there was the time difference and he hadn't left any messages on my phone so I decided not to. I was trying to get back to my husband by way of Maine, which was the long, long way home. It no longer made sense, but I'd promised my mother. The girls and I got up and ate cereal, and Ginny drove us to the airport.

68

All three of us slept on the plane to Newark. We were supposed to take a smaller plane from Newark to Boston but the winds were too strong and the plane got delayed, which was hard on Myla and she lay down on the carpet by the gate. Elisabeth said her stomach hurt then, and she began to cry and couldn't get relief, but when we finally boarded, she seemed fine. Before we took off, the pilot told us he was ordering the flight attendants to stay in their seats for the duration because the ride would be very bumpy. I was in the aisle seat and tried to hide my worry over this, but Myla was in the middle next to me and saw me put my face in my hands.

When the plane took off, we slammed against something like a wall of wind or an expanse of steel. "Why in God's name are we doing this?" I said.

"Are you scared, Mama?" Myla asked.

"I'm scared." The moment was quick, but I think she saw it—that I was a person separate from her, and that my fear was different than her fear, and this quieted her for a little while.

We landed in Boston at ten-thirty at night and were meant to take the last bus to Portland and sleep at the Embassy Suites near the airport, then rent a car in the morning and drive to my mother. It was Friday of Fourth of July and traffic got backed up around Logan for miles, and many people milled around the terminal in the dark waiting for the bus, and when it finally came, there was a rush, but we got seats—Myla in the aisle behind Elisabeth and me.

We made it to my mother's around noon the next day, and I slept in my old room, and the girls slept in Ginny's room, and no one slept in Margaret's room. The light changed while we were asleep, and when I woke up it was four in the afternoon and it became an undertaking to care for my girls and be responsive to my mother.

My father had died from a stroke five years earlier, and my mother lived alone, and each time I came home this took me time to get used to. Before he'd died I'd wanted to forgive my father for the bank teller named Tammy Plover, but I'd been too young. Then my feelings about what he did hardened, and the thought of Tammy Plover angered me. I'm aware now that anger isn't really an emotion and that being mad at my father is a way of keeping him alive longer, and I miss him.

The landing at the top of the stairs had an old blue-and-white braided rug on it, and Margaret and I used to sit on this rug in the afternoons and read. My girls now stood on the rug on their way down the stairs, and Myla asked Elisabeth, "Who do you love?"

"I only love Mom and Dad."

"Me too," Myla said. "Only Mom and Dad."

The house was like the pilothouse on top of a ship meant to withstand winds and high seas. Pine floors and recessed lights and small square windows. But everything had shrunk—the banister and stairs and the kitchen and the yard and the cabin in the woods behind the yard. The floorboards were wider in the kitchen and warped closer to the sink where my mother stood peeling potatoes, her hair in a loose white-gray bun. The girls ran out the back door and tried to teach themselves how to throw a Frisbee, and my mother got out hamburger from the fridge, and I opened it and put it in the bowl she handed me and chopped the green onion.

I wanted to tell her about Alcatraz, and the man on Fisherman's Wharf behind the bush, but I didn't know how to begin. I feared she would make me feel bad for getting into these situations in the first place, because she could do that. When the meatloaf was done she called the girls in, and they sat at the table by the window that looked down over the driveway she'd recently gotten tarred.

"Robert," she said after she'd sat down. My father had been dead five years. "Robert, I forget where you said I put the salt."

I watched her stand and circle the kitchen not knowing where she was exactly. She found the salt and sat down again, and we prayed. I was again afraid that the girls would refuse to go through with it, but we held hands and bowed our heads.

69

Later that week we drove to Pemaquid Beach and walked past the clearing with the charcoal grates and picnic tables I'd seen in my mind on the wall in China. We put our blankets on the sand. The urge I'd had to drink seemed further away here. The idea of drinking was still something chemical in me, but also the memory of an obligation. I'm not sure I can explain it. When you drink, you're in a private conversation with the drinking, and it becomes something you do, and in this way it's an obligation. A gift you give yourself, but also a weapon.

I knew an American painter who came to Beijing for a show I'd helped organize before I had the girls, and I met her at the airport and drove her around the city. The woman was interested in the things involved with Tibetan altars—the brass bell and pestle and mortar. She asked me to drive her to the shops and markets that might have these altarpieces, and while I drove, she pulled a silver flask out of her shoulder bag and took sips. She did this regularly throughout the day so when it came time to give her talk at the gallery in Dashanzi, I thought she'd be quite drunk, but instead she'd just maintained her obligation to the drinking. She spoke well about her painting process and slurred her words only a little.

In Maine my drinking was the memory of an obligation. I'll say that it was also a lost friend. Maybe a friend who wanted to cause me great harm, but still a friend. When you're lonely and unable to be alone with yourself, you're glad for any friend. It took up a great deal of my thinking during the time I was in a relationship with it.

There were kayaks for rent at the beach, and I asked Elisabeth if she wanted to go out in one with me, and she shook her head. "I'm not a kayak person. When will you ever understand that?" I tried not to laugh, and we walked back to our blankets, and the girls and my mother built a small fort out of driftwood, large enough for the girls to stand in.

I clapped for them from where I stood in the water and went for a long swim back and forth along the beach, maybe twenty feet out, and it was cold and lovely.

When I dried off, Myla said, "That made me uneasy, Mama. To see you swimming out there alone."

I nodded and took in her worry, and this time on the beach was the real beginning of my understanding how to be with her fully.

70

That night Elisabeth began having stomach pains. Mild at first and then sharper. We were on the couch in the living room where my mother had installed a brown recliner to watch TV in. This chair, like the tarring of the driveway, was a surprise because my mother hated tarred driveways when we were growing up, and hated TV more.

I sat with Elisabeth and Myla and didn't talk to my mother about Margaret, even though this was the subject she most warmed to. Elisabeth's head was in my lap, and I asked if she thought she might need to make a poop, and she moaned. I took her in my arms and rocked her and my mother got her a wet washcloth for her forehead, and at eight o'clock I walked both girls to bed.

Elisabeth came to me at four in the morning and said her stomach hurt more, and I gave her Tylenol and put her back to bed. At six she crawled in with me and held her stomach, and I tried to touch where it hurt but she wouldn't let me. Myla woke up and looked worried, and I wanted to spare her so I told her to go ask her grandmother for cereal. "Do you think you can do that? Go wake your grandmother up on your own?"

She said yes she could, and she did as she was told.

Then Elisabeth threw up in my bed. She'd been outside playing all week, and I thought she was dehydrated. I helped her walk to the bathroom and cleaned her face with a washcloth, and when I kissed her she was burning. We got back in bed, and she closed her eyes, and I used the phone next to the bed to leave a message at the doctor's office in Augusta.

Twenty minutes later my mother yelled up from the kitchen. "Doctor on the phone!"

The nurse asked me Elisabeth's symptoms.

"She now has a very bad headache."

"What happens when you try to palpate her stomach where the pain is?"

I put the receiver down and tried to press the area of Elisabeth's stomach where the pain was worse, and she screamed.

"I can't do it," I said into the phone. "It hurts her too much."

"Take her in. You can't be sure. Sounds like appendix and I'd take her in."

71

The ambulance had to turn around at the end of our drive-way, and the overgrown pine trees made it tight. I didn't think they were going to make it, and I said this out loud. The driver was a volunteer firefighter named Spike I'd known all my life. He owned the one gas station in town and smiled at me through his open window and said, "Elsey. Turning this thing around is not our biggest problem here."

Then he parked and got out and opened the back doors so he and an EMT named Dane could put Elisabeth's stretcher in. My mother stood on the front porch holding Myla's shoulders, and I willed Myla not to have one of her fits over me leaving. I went to her and told her she would be okay with her grandma, and I kissed her face and she stared at Elisabeth on the stretcher, and my mother did the smart thing and took her inside.

I climbed into the ambulance and sat on one side of Dane. A nurse named Noreen sat on Dane's other side, and I followed Dane's instructions to keep talking to Elisabeth while

Noreen put the IV needle into the vein on top of my daughter's hand. Then Elisabeth began screaming in a way I hadn't heard before, and Spike put the sirens on, and we drove through road construction on the bridge into Augusta with more construction on Wayland Road.

Elisabeth went through two bags of fluid and kept throwing up until there was black bile in the bin that Noreen asked me to hold under her mouth.

"We're all thinking appendix," Dane said.

"The fever is the clue," Noreen said.

They were good people, Dane and Noreen. They did not talk down to Elisabeth. They spoke to her like she was a person, and Noreen said that an appendix was a ticking clock and told Spike to drive faster.

"I don't know what hurts more, the IV or my stomach," Elisabeth whispered to me and cried more, because something had gone wrong with the IV needle and it pressed into her wrong.

"Take it out! Please take it out. Please, Mama, take it out."

I told her if she could just wait the doctor would fix it. I said, "I love you."

I kept repeating that. That I loved her and that we would get the IV out.

The emergency room was brightly lit, with a semicircle of six examining rooms with glass doors. Dane wheeled Elisabeth into the second room on the right if you were looking from the nurses' desk, and one of the nurses followed us into the room and asked me Elisabeth's weight. I didn't know it. I didn't know her height, either. I could guess, and it turned out I was close, but I didn't know exact measurements. Lukas would have known them.

The nurse's name was Angie, and she wore purple clogs and said she needed to give Elisabeth morphine for her pain and what was Elisabeth's blood type? I didn't know that, either. A woman from the hospital administration office came in and said she needed to know Elisabeth's Social Security number. She was seven, I said, and I hadn't memorized it yet. I wondered how many other things they would ask me about my daughter that I wouldn't know the answer to.

I left Lukas two messages on his phone, and each one said call me. Call me please as soon as you can. After the woman from the administration office finished, I called him again and said, "Elisabeth is sick. Elisabeth is in the hospital. Oh, Lukas, I am so sorry. Oh, Lukas, call me."

There was a male patient two doors down from Elisabeth's room who started screaming, and I think this acted on each of us in the ER differently. The man sounded horribly sad, as if he didn't have any hope, and what a thing.

Then a doctor came into Elisabeth's room and said his name was Howard Swan and that the clock was ticking on Ms. Elisabeth. "Twelve hours after the pain starts," Dr. Swan said. He wore small, round wire glasses. "Then the appendix has to come out."

An hour later they wheeled her into the OR and prepped her for surgery. She reminded me of a deer. Not a fawn. Or a grown deer. But maybe a teenage deer. Everything about her was brown—her wild hair, her darker eyebrows and skin from the beach. I thought all of these were Lukas.

72

When it was almost time, Elisabeth looked up and asked me to come into the operating room with her. "Of course," I said. I don't know why I hadn't thought of it earlier or why none of the nurses had offered.

A nurse rushed me to a metal locker, and I put on a white bunny suit made of crepe paper, and a blue skullcap and facemask like the nurses and surgeon wore, and I went back to Elisabeth's bed and took her hand and told her again that I loved her.

"Did it hurt when you had your surgery?" she asked. I thought she was too young to have registered anything about my thyroid, and we'd never talked about it. "Did it hurt?"

"No." I was casual, because she was scared and this had to be casual. "No, it didn't hurt. The surgery didn't hurt."

"Don't lie to me."

"I'm not lying, Elisabeth." I meant this. "I love you. Daddy loves you. Myla loves you."

Another nurse named Sue said we were on our way to the

place where they made the incisions, and Elisabeth liked this word, incisions, and she repeated it.

"Incisions," she said again while they wheeled her in, and I kept holding her hand.

The act of wheeling her into the OR caused the IV needle to move, and tears leaked down her face. "We are here with you. I am here with you. Daddy's here with you. Myla's here with you. I love you." I said this. It was the only thing I could think of to say that mattered.

Sue put a green facemask over my daughter's face that looked like it had a snorkel attached, and she instructed Elisabeth to breathe in until her lungs were full. When Sue took the mask away, Elisabeth said, "I have a statement to make. Whispering is like black and white. Speaking is like color."

Her eyes crossed briefly and she was gone. Then one of the other nurses asked me to leave, and I couldn't believe she was asking me to do this.

"I have kids," Dr. Swan said, because he was reading my mind. I bet none of the parents want to leave, because how could you want to? "We all have kids in this room."

But even before he said this, I felt their big-heartedness and was leaving the room.

· 73 ·

I walked to the waiting area with the blue poster of Cinque
Terre on the Italian coast, and I called Lukas three more
times and the third time he picked up and told me things that
helped me understand that Elisabeth would live. He also said
he loved me and was so sorry he'd been sleeping when I'd
called before and could I tell him more about Elisabeth's vital
signs and how long the nurses thought the surgery would
take?

We talked many times during the surgery. I've lost count,
and each time we talked, I had more things to tell him about
Elisabeth and I tried to remember everything so he could
feel like he was there with us.

At the end of one of the calls Lukas said, "When are you
coming back?"

"As soon as Elisabeth is able to fly."

"I'll be the man with a beard at the airport and a sign that
reads 'Elsey come home. Elsey, Elisabeth and Myla come
home.'"

He was trying to distract me, and it worked and I laughed and hung up. Then I was alone in the waiting room and went to the time of Margaret at the hospitals when she called on me and called on me for water and Coke and sourballs. Then the surgery was over, and they wheeled Elisabeth into the room with the pink curtain, and she didn't wake up for a long time.

Two hours went by while I sat next to her bed.

"Elisabeth." The nurse named Betty wiggled the toes on her right foot with her hand. "Elisabeth, are you in there?"

She didn't move. After each hour I called Lukas and called my mother and told them not to worry.

"Elisabeth," Betty said after four hours had gone by. "Come in, please, Elisabeth."

It was the most dreamlike part. She looked fine but she wasn't with us.

When she finally opened her eyes, Betty asked, "Where are you, Elisabeth?"

"I'm in the place where they do incisions."

Then she went back to sleep.

The next time she woke up, she was in her own bed in a pale green hospital room, and I was holding her hand. "Do I have to ever go to another circus?"

"No you do not." Had I been forcing her to circuses? We'd gone to two. I smiled and tried to remember to tell Lukas.

"Good. That's a relief. I don't like the clowns."

· 74 ·

We got to my mother's house two days later, and Myla was solemn when we carried Elisabeth in. I'd never seen Myla able to hold herself together so completely, and I was grateful for that and for my mother. I put Elisabeth in my double bed so I could watch her, and I put Myla in Ginny's bed.

Once they were asleep, I went into Margaret's room, which was the only room in the house with a slatted wooden ceiling like the floor of a ship. Her bed had three fish carved into the headboard, and I could hear trees and birds outside the window. I felt clear. When you're in the hospital with a small girl, everything becomes clear. It really does.

It was quiet in the house, and my mother had also gone to sleep early. I didn't stay in my sister's room long, but I felt like myself in there and not terribly lonely like I had after she was gone. I haven't written that Elisabeth has Margaret's long face, and Myla has Margaret's long arms and legs. I sat on my sister's bed and told her Elisabeth wasn't going to die, and that I'd never believed she was going to die. I said I hadn't believed that she, Margaret, was ever going to die, either, and I always thought I'd see her again and I missed her.

Ginny was too young and had been sent to my mother's parents in Augusta during the worst part, and I'd been less than vigilant until then. I had my pot and my running and my music, and it was the surprise of it that still got me. I'd come and gone to school and cross-country practice and studied my face in the mirror. I was already getting ready to leave Hallowell. I had great excitement inside me over this, and I thought my sister would live as long into the future as I could see. So the difference was everything. They put her on a stretcher and wheeled her to the top of the landing, and two men carried her down the eighteen stairs.

She was my charge. I mean, there were nurses in the last months and there were my parents, but I thought of her as mine. I'd made her mine the way an older sister does, and she was so agreeable to it. I was also embarrassed for having not known. The joke was on me with my running practices and my thin, poorly rolled joints, and my misunderstanding. I never thought she would die, and it has taken me until now to stop trying to resolve the joke. There are people who aren't trying to solve the joke. Mei was like this, and I learned from her. Things came up. She let them go.

Myla and Elisabeth were sleeping in rooms down the hall, and I was their mother and I needed to go check on them. I said goodbye to my sister out loud. It wasn't weighted with meaning, and I didn't imply I'd be back, because I didn't think I would be. Margaret listened in her even way and I left her.

75

Two weeks later we made an unplanned landing near a small city west of Beijing and sat on the runway waiting out a lightning storm. There was no way of knowing how long we'd be there. The flight attendants weren't interested in giving out information, and I began texting my husband: We are close but still so far away and do you love me?

The girls lay on top of each other in their seats, and opened and closed their eyes. Their faces were sweaty and they didn't speak. It was hot on the plane because they'd had to turn off the engines in the storm, and the toilets were also out of order. The flight attendants offered each passenger a small glass bottle of vodka for free while we waited. The bottles were clear with little metallic blue tops, and arranged on the drink cart like toys that people opened and drank with or without the melting ice in plastic cups.

I didn't reach for a bottle when the flight attendant came to my row with her cart and offered me one, but I did think about it. Then I texted my husband again from the field. I was so sorry for the things I'd put us through: I have no idea where we are or when we'll get to you. Will you ever forgive me?

I wrote that I still had pain in my arm, and promised myself I'd have it checked and later I did, and he was right. It was a nerve tear, and with physical therapy it got better.

Lukas wrote back: At arrivals already.

There was the long line at Immigration, and after thirty minutes or so we cleared and walked down the white hall to the luggage carousels. After customs, we passed through the automatic doors that opened to the international terminal, where there was always a throng. People pushed up against the metal gate and tried to see, and they called the names of their people, but the metal gate held us back, and Lukas couldn't get to us.

I scanned for him and finally found him to the right of the gate holding the sign, and the girls saw him and ran and threw themselves at his legs, and he laughed and kissed me and took my hand. Once we were sorted in the car, he told me he'd gotten the dryer fixed and I laughed at that, too, and sometimes this is all it takes.

I looked at my husband's face in the car, and the long, curly beard told a story. I'll never leave you. This is what I thought while I watched Lukas drive us home from the airport. I'll never leave you again. Who knows if this was even true, but it felt true to me.

In the car, he told the girls that one-quarter of the hutong behind our apartment had been razed by bulldozers. "I stood in our bedroom window and watched the demolition for hours. I was worried. Very, very worried about this turn of events. Then a low structure began to go up. Tin corrugated roof. Metal siding. I'd expected a high-rise. Or a storage facility or airplane hangar." He looked at me. "Kids ran in and out of its front door, which was a garage door made of steel. So I walked over one morning. And Myla"—Lukas paused for effect—"you will not believe it. It's a place for farmers to bring their vegetables and meat."

Myla clapped and Elisabeth laughed and I smiled, and I think in Lukas's mind the hutong had been saved and so had our marriage. We got back to the apartment and the girls wanted to sleep in Elisabeth's bunk beds. Lukas wrestled with them on the rug and hugged them tightly and put Myla on the top and Elisabeth on the bottom, and no one argued. They were too tired.

He and I stayed up in the living room looking out the windows at the city, and when we went to bed, it was almost two in the morning. We could see hundreds of skyscrapers out our window and many cranes, but not the most enormous skyscraper that's like a pair of huge pants. You can see that only from Elisabeth's room. I told him how I'd said good-bye to my sister in her room in Hallowell, and that this sat underneath everything and that for a very long time I'd been waiting for her to come back, but I wasn't as much now.

"That's good," he said. "Remember. That's only normal."

We made love, and it was tender, and I think I closed my eyes afterward but was too tired and excited to sleep.

76

I learned later that week that Justice's father who owned the bookstore had vanished and was released by the police but sworn not to speak of it or sell subversive books at the store any longer. I worried for Mei, and Lukas worried, too. I called Justice. Neither of us had heard from her. I texted her often, and she didn't text back. I told myself she was probably safe and that our friendship was over, but I couldn't understand if it was or wasn't, and if not texting back meant a friendship hadn't amounted to anything in the end. Texting seemed like a poor test of what she'd meant to me.

Lukas and I wrote our ambassador in China and called a friend who was friends with the assistant to the ambassador. A journalist from the New York Times wrote an op-ed piece on Mei and where she might be. Then I finally got an email in September from someone called LittleBunny, who asked if I could do a handstand yet.

She wrote that she'd been sick with a blood disease while she was in jail, but that it was a sickness she'd known she had for several years, so she was not worried. "Why," she also wrote, "do people who are not sick think sick people are soldiers when really we are just sick people who are not obligated to come back from the front lines to report on our sickness so healthy people can feel better?"

The police had come for her a few weeks after they'd taken Justice's father, and they released her in a small city near Shanghai, but she'd traveled back to Chengdu to be with another cousin because, she wrote, she could not be alone.

She did not want me to visit, because if I saw her I would pity her. But Lukas agreed I should go right away, and I flew to Chengdu and met her at a dumpling house where dead flies stuck to strips of sticky paper on the wall. She was so thin. I wanted to ask about the jail and if Leng had come for her, but I didn't want to upset her. She told me she'd begun to see ghosts, but that was all she said about her time in jail, and I think if I'd asked more, she would have forbidden me. She was close to cutting off contact with people she knew, including me. I could feel it—that she was moving away, and I think it was part of her long disease, to go through this phase.

"Your sickness," I said. "It sounds very serious, and you should have told me earlier. I could have helped." I took a sip of tea and watched to see how much she'd let me in. "Could we please talk about the medicines you need?"

"What is really 'very serious'?" She laughed and made the sign for quotation marks with her fingers. "I tell you about my disease, and you think I am the victim now. No." She hit the table with her hand and pointed her cigarette at me, and I was overcome by emotion—the kind I'd had with her in Shashan and didn't know how to name.

She wasn't self-conscious at all. "I want to be the heroine of my story. And you, too, Elsey. You, too, be the heroine. Not the victim. Understand? Because the heroine is the one who owns the story."

She is still my favorite person in the world after the two little girls and the Danish man I live with in Beijing. She's recovering, and she paints and has made a life in Chengdu as a critic of corruption. When I see her, she is like family and remains opaque.

77

The Alcoholics Anonymous meetings I went to that summer were in a stone community center in Shunyi that used to be a traditional courtyard house. The center offered yoga and cooking classes and Zumba, and this is where I talked about the distance the drinking gave me. There were rooms for massage in the back and an open studio in front where they offered watercolor classes, and where I later taught portrait classes, which were kind of a disaster, but that isn't part of this story.

A Chinese woman named Iris taught the yoga classes, and she is my friend now. But back then Iris sat on the white couch with her students after their yoga class, and they laughed and I wanted so much to sit with them, but I went into the conference room in the back of the center and listened to the alcoholics.

These meetings were a production to get to. The center was on a dirt road behind a hutong that had no real address, and each time I took a cab out there, it was difficult to find.

One time the cabdriver fell asleep while he was driving, and I had to scream and hit his arm to wake him up and I've not gotten over that feeling of having no control.

There were usually six of us, led by an Australian woman named Nan who'd followed her husband to China for his work doing economic assessment at the United Nations. Nan had once gotten very drunk at an expat networking dinner I'd been to years before and had to be taken out of the Hyatt by her husband. It was embarrassing to watch, and I remember feeling certain I'd never come as undone as she was.

I can't talk some people into the fact that I have a drinking problem because they don't want to believe it. At the Alcoholics Anonymous meetings in Shunyi, people didn't have to be convinced. I've disappointed other people I know, not through my drinking or passing out while the girls were in their beds, but through my unwillingness to continue to drink with them.

I went to these meetings in Shunyi almost every day for six months, and I think they saved my life. I know they saved my marriage. I still go because they teach me words for how I feel, and this is why I'm finally more available to my girls. It is ongoing.

78

It's been helpful to write this account, and now I almost don't want to stop. I've recently begun a series of paintings of women standing outside Beijing construction projects and by canals and city parks. I give each person an attribute: a bright red purse. A green sweater. I go to the studio several mornings a week and the subject is the people, and if there's anything implied about point of view it's of a person who doesn't have the right to speak on China, really.

I try to be reckless when I'm making the paintings, which is really at odds with having the girls, and I bring the paintings home when I'm done with them. I don't keep them separate from my other life, or let them be precious. I hang them in the living room and dining room, and try not to have two lives, or keep count of the time I spend in each life. It's not always simple, and sometimes things compete and I let the girls devour me or let the painting take over. These are bad days, and I know to look for them.

Bree, my art dealer, has set up a show for me this fall in

London at a small gallery in Chelsea. We'll all go together, Lukas and the girls and me, and this makes me very happy. I think Ginny and my mother will meet us in London, which will be a big trip for my mother, and I'm grateful to Ginny for flying to Maine and gathering her. Ginny and I have decided (mostly Ginny has decided) that in London my mother will be offered the choice to move to San Francisco and live in Ginny's basement or live in a retirement home in Augusta. I know she won't like either choice, and I know which one I'd pick, but I can't be sure with my mother.

Last night Elisabeth threw some pasta in the air and tried to catch it in her mouth, and I asked her to please bring a sponge from the kitchen, and she stood by the table and stared at my painting on the wall and said I'd painted the policemen's uniforms wrong. It was as if she'd never seen the painting before, though it had been hanging there for weeks: dozens of women and kids outside the Temple of Heaven walking in different directions bending toward hope, while the policemen stand by watching.

"Come eat, pet," Lukas said. "Maybe your mom doesn't care so much about the uniforms."

He looked at me across the table and waited to see what I'd say. We're vigilant about the distance between us and don't let it get too large, which requires more naming of emotion than I've known. This is awkward sometimes and formulaic and sort of like the Talking Circle. The audience for his music grows, and he flies to the festivals and sometimes we go with him and sometimes not, and then I don't let the solitude become something that feels permanent or has substance that could harm me.

Myla banged her fork down on the table. "Elisabeth's right. The policemen's hats are done wrong."

Elisabeth nodded dramatically, and how did she already know about this effect? She made her way to Lukas's lap and reached for the udon in his bowl and ate it with her hands. "I hope you don't think you're done with that painting, Mom. I hope it's just practice. I can help you. I know how to do hats. It's easy." Elisabeth still tells me that when she describes certain things to me about her imagination, I sometimes smile my fake mommy smile, but this wasn't my fake smile.

"I'll take lessons from you and Myla. Please let me know when we can arrange that."

It's been only a year since Shashan, and when it seems like nothing has changed it takes a day or two before I'm better. Lukas told me recently that he knows me and has always known me, and there's great relief for me in being seen like this. I believe what he says, but I've had to explain to him that knowing me doesn't mean he has to do everything for me, and that I'm competent. He's had to really listen to this part, and I think he understands what I mean but it's hard for him to wait, and sometimes I still don't talk much even when he waits and that's okay.

The girls left the table and went into the living room to run back and forth on the couch in their bare feet. Running and running. Lukas and I watched from the table, and I felt something substantial press inside me I'll call the understanding of a precarious happiness. It wasn't too much. I saw what the rest of a life could be like with this happiness, and then it began to rain and it hardly ever rains in China and each time it does I take it as a good sign. I stood and moved to the empty chair beside my husband, and the girls finished running and fell down on the couch laughing.

Acknowledgments

Enormous gratitude to my incredibly wise editor, Carole Baron. I'm a very lucky woman to get to work with her again and a better writer for knowing her. It's been one of the great gifts of my life. Thanks also to the supremely talented Genevieve Nierman and Jenny Carrow and to everyone at Knopf. I also bow down to my dear agent extraordinaire, Stephanie Cabot, for steering this project. I'm indebted to everyone at the Gernert Agency. Such heartfelt thanks to my invaluable first readers and trusted ones: Lily King, Caitlin Gutheil, Anja Hanson, Lewis Robinson, Sara Corbett, Katie Longstreth, Elisabeth Dekker, Desi Van Til, Maryanne O'Hara and Caitlin Shetterly. To my brother, sister, and parent Conleys, big love and thanks. And to my colleagues at the Stonecoast MFA program, whom I'm lucky to get to learn from.